After the hectic routine of St Vincent's, life in the sick-bay of Leisure TV seems tame to Sister Penny Shepherd. Until, that is, she's asked to become medical adviser to a new series, *Life Lines*, and finds herself in constant battle with its autocratic presenter, Dr Justin Welles . . .

LIFE LINES

BY
MEG WISGATE

MILLS & BOON LIMITED
London · Sydney · Toronto

First published in Great Britain 1984
by Mills & Boon Limited, 15–16 Brook's Mews,
London W1A 1DR

ISBN 0 263 74813 8

Set in 10 on 12 pt Linotron Times
03/0884

Photoset by Rowland Phototypesetting Ltd
Bury St Edmunds, Suffolk
Made and printed in Great Britain by
Richard Clay (The Chaucer Press) Ltd
Bungay, Suffolk

CHAPTER ONE

IT WAS one of those uncertain yet promising days, when April's last rains were being ushered out by the growing warmth of the sun. Droplets from the most recent shower were already disappearing from the black bodywork of the passing taxis and the hiss of bus tyres was fading as the wet London streets began to dry. Umbrellas were being shaken and folded by the lunchtime throng as they resumed their progress along the pavements and occasionally cast optimistic glances up at the patches of blue sky which were increasingly visible above the tall buildings. There was more than a hint of spring in the air.

There was, however, less than a hint of spring in Sister Penny Shepherd's hurried step. She collapsed her slinger umbrella as well, gave it a shake and slipped its strap over her shoulder. She glanced at her watch. Comfortably in time for the end of her lunch break, she decided, and slowed her pace to more of a saunter. A couple of office juniors overtook her, chattering animatedly, teenage legs striding easily along beneath short hemlines.

Penny frowned slightly. She really should have bought that dress in the Bond Street store she had just left. The assistant had almost persuaded her, she mused—had said she had the figure to carry it off, that it really suited her and so forth—but something within had decided her to leave it. Somehow the dress required a certain light-heartedness which she could not find in the reflection of her face in the changing-room mirror.

She could not pick out any real reason for the glumness she felt, other than a faint dissatisfaction with the way her new job as sick-bay sister at Leisure Television had turned out. Clive had painted such an attractive picture of it when she had applied for the position and it had certainly seemed an exciting contrast to men's surgical at St Vincent's. But then Clive had a knack of making things appear larger than life, she recalled with a fond smile, as she turned down a side street towards the imposing headquarters of LTV. It was not so much that the job was dreary—it was just that it all seemed rather, well, superficial. Running medical screening tests on staff, dispensing analgesics to cure headaches and supervising an after-hours keep-fit class seemed hardly enough to occupy her time, and she realised she was missing the real demands that had been made on her at St Vincent's.

Deep in thought, she reached Strand Tower and stepped up and across the paved patio leading to the entrance. Even the raised flower beds with their breathtaking displays of bright yellow daffodils failed to catch her attention. She stepped into a segment of the revolving doors and pressed her hand against the glass panel.

With sudden force it swung away from her. Taken completely unawares, she stopped in her tracks, her slinger umbrella slipping from her shoulder. Its handle fell back and infuriatingly jammed between the door's edge and the next glass panel. The revolving doors ceased revolving with an angry sort of crunch.

Feeling rather silly and not unlike something trapped in a glass cage, she turned to retrieve the umbrella. Barely had she straightened from picking it up than the doors began to revolve in the opposite direction, again with considerable speed, and she felt herself being expelled back out on to the paved patio in a manner resembling a bullet being fired from a gun. Utterly furious by now, she turned to seek the cause of all this unnecessary force—obviously someone who saw revolving doors as an obstacle requiring frontal assault, rather than a convenient and simple method of leaving a building. She glared at the tall male figure which was appearing through the smoked glass and nonchalantly stepping out on to the paving.

The words of protest died in her throat as a pair of quite extraordinarily piercing blue eyes seized hers.

'You appear to be having some trouble with your accessories,' he observed in tones of mild amusement, eyeing her umbrella.

Penny gaped at this display of patronising audacity. She sought to control her feelings and return the supercilious stare but her gaze quite unaccountably failed to hold his. In confusion, she found a diversion in her brolly and brandished it at him, handle first.

'Look what you've done to it,' she demanded angrily. 'The handle's ruined!'

An expression of concern flitted across the fine brow and an eyebrow arched in surprise. 'Oh, surely not,' he said. 'Let me look.'

He reached out and grasped it firmly, withdrawing it from her hand. She had no choice but to let him take it and felt strangely defenceless as she stood before him, awkward and cross.

It was almost as if he sensed her feeling of inadequacy, for he stared at her again, this time letting his gaze travel down from the collar of her dark mac to her slim ankles in the black court shoes. It was not a look so frank as to give offence, but it was disturbing. He returned his attention to her umbrella and closely inspected the handle.

'I don't think it's ruined exactly,' he announced, the irony in his voice barely concealed. 'You have dented the wood and the lacquer is crazed, but I rather think,' he applied some pressure to the handle joint, 'that there is no evidence of a fracture—merely a mild abrasion.'

He regarded her quizzically and again she felt the most extraordinary jolt as his eyes seared into hers. How odd that he should use a medical turn of phrase. It was as though he knew she was wearing a white uniform beneath the mac and was making fun of her. Her eyes dropped involuntarily to check, but the buttons were all done up and she was wearing a blue silk scarf at her throat which she knew obscured the top. This was ridiculous. She took a breath and looked back up at him, determined to call a halt to this absurd scene.

He had reversed his wrist and was holding the umbrella out at an angle, for all the world like an épée. She quickly blinked away this outrageous notion.

'A very fashionable design,' he observed. 'But a little unwieldy. Myself, I prefer something rather more compact and practical.'

She saw that he was carrying an elegant, stubby umbrella of the telescopic variety, which he held up for her to see, an expression of insufferable superiority on his face.

Again, she fumbled for some suitably dismissive reply. Suddenly the confusion within her was compounded even further as she felt the most powerful conviction that they had met somewhere before. There was something strangely familiar about the face that confronted her, something about the distinctive head of crinkly black hair, the lean, handsome features and the firm jaw. She realised she was staring at him like some vacant half-wit.

His eyes, however, had been closely examing the details of her face and now seemed to be intently studying her figure. Again she felt a strong sense of disquiet. Her heart appeared to be thudding at a level far out of proportion to the importance of the situation. She seized upon attack as her best form of defence.

'I dare say you do need to carry a folding umbrella,' she observed icily, head tilted back in a vain attempt to look down upon features that were nearly a head taller than hers. 'I imagine you have to travel light—in view of the speed and total lack of regard for others which you maintain.' He was looking at her in amazement.

She plunged on, unable to stop. 'Personally, I usually check whether other people are trying to enter doorways when I use them, particularly revolving doorways.'

'Yes,' he replied, nodding slowly and with studied agreement. 'Yes, I can see that. Well, if you're quite sure your umbrella is not irretrievably damaged . . .' Without waiting for a reply, he neatly flipped her umbrella end to end and proffered her the handle. She was obliged to accept it.

'Good-afternoon.' He afforded her a courteous, but almost imperceptible bow from the waist, sidestepped and strode past her across the paving and down on to the busy street, to slide smoothly into the back of one of LTV's limousines drawn up at the kerb. A uniformed chauffeur pushed shut the car door.

She stared after him for a moment and then, aware that she must appear faintly ridiculous standing stock-still in the entrance-way and gawping across the street, she gave a shake of her head and moved on and in through the doors, this time with no mishap.

She made her way over to the bank of lifts at the opposite end of LTV's spacious entrance lobby. Halfway across, she noticed that George, one of the company's security commissionaires, was twinkling at her from behind his desk in the corner.

'Bit of a whirlwind, that one,' he observed with a grin.

'You can say that again, George,' agreed Penny. 'Not exactly an upholder of old-world chivalry and charm, either.' She paused and, curiosity driving her, stepped over to the desk. 'He nearly turned the revolving doors into a food-mixer—with me as the ingredients!'

'Yes, Sister, I saw. But to give him his due, he wasn't really thinking—a bit distracted by handshakes and farewells from Jeremy Wheeler. I think they'd both been up at a special VIP lunch in the hospitality suite.'

'Jeremy Wheeler, eh?' said Penny in surprise. 'The head of documentaries doesn't personally come down to see *every* guest off the premises. He must have been quite an important visitor.' She realised with a guilty start that she was leaning over George's desk, trying to decipher the signatures in his visitor's register—but George turned the book round so she could see. He indicated a flamboyant scrawl amongst the pre-lunch arrivals.

'Justin Welles,' she read. Such was the flourish that it took up two complete lines on the page. 'Typical,' she muttered.

'Doesn't mean anything to me, Sister,' shrugged George.

'Nor me,' acknowledged Penny lightly, but something still tugged at her memory, a vague familiarity she could not pin down.

She straightened up abruptly. Enough of this pointless conjecture. She returned George's shrug and went over to the lifts again, joining the crowd of staff returning from lunch.

Up in her sick-bay, she hung up her mac and quickly changed back into the white shoes she wore on duty. A quick trip to the cloakroom that formed part of her domain sufficed to check her hair and make-up. She surveyed herself in a mirror for the second time that lunch-hour and tucked a few wayward strands of ash blonde hair into the neat coiffure she adopted for work. Wearing her hair up was not the ideal style to balance her rather wide forehead and she much preferred to wear it brushed out and shoulder length. Making the best of herself whilst still conforming to the formal styles required by her profession had always been something of a problem, she acknowledged ruefully, and leaned forward to reapply a touch of the natural pink lipstick which she favoured.

She was not a girl given to airs and graces and had the honest background of being a Sussex farmer's daughter. She would have been the last person, for example, to observe that the breadth of her features was more than compensated for by the fullness of her mouth, with its promise of warm passions within. Her friends, who frequently saw her in laughing mood, would have said the smile on her lips seemed to light up her entire face and reflect in the flashing white teeth and soft grey eyes. It could be infectious, to say the least.

At the moment though, she exuded an air of quiet

efficiency and, giving her belt a tweak and straightening the line of her white apron, she returned to her office to review the activities scheduled for that Friday afternoon.

The p.m. page of her appointments diary stared blankly and depressingly back at her and she remembered gloomily that she had allocated the afternoon to administration. There was not even a medical screening to be done. She did enjoy these, especially if they involved people from the programme staff of LTV, who were invariably entertaining and good fun. They always told her anecdotes about the show business personalities they worked with and the hilarious disasters which occasionally occurred and which the viewer at home never saw. But there were to be no diversions that afternoon.

With customary resolve, she picked up the papers in her in-tray. Part of her duties were to sit on LTV's staff welfare committee and she settled down to read the rather lengthy and extremely dull minutes from the last meeting. She was about halfway through when the internal phone shrilled. She picked it up, glad of the distraction.

'Sister Shepherd,' she answered.

'Oh Sister, it's Remington here, financial accounts. We've got something of a problem here—one of the clerks has badly sprained her wrist. Silly girl had opened all four drawers in a filing cabinet at the same time. I'm always telling them. Anyway, the cabinet started to tilt over, she tried to step out of the way and fell awkwardly. I don't think it's serious, but there are a lot of tears and—'

'Where is the girl now?' interrupted Penny firmly.

'Well actually she's on her way down to you. My secretary's bringing her.'

'And her name?'

'Manning, Carole Manning.'

'Right, Mr Remington. I'll be expecting her.' She replaced the receiver and went over to her records file, flicking through the pockets until she came to M.

Here it was. Carole Manning. She pulled out the A4 folder and checked the details. First job, seventeen years old, junior clerk. Penny remembered her now, recalled her coming for her medical checks, all shyness and nervous giggles.

There were no giggles from the white-faced youngster who came through the outer door of the sick-bay a few moments later, supported weakly on the arm of a very concerned-looking secretary. Carole's eyes were smudged where she had wiped tears away along with her mascara and she was obviously in some pain.

'Well, what have we here?' enquired Penny lightly. 'Come along, let's have a look at you.' She manoeuvred the two of them into one of her examination cubicles, careful not to jog the arm that Carole was gripping tightly with her other hand.

'I'm so glad to have got her down here, Sister,' said the secretary. 'I really thought she was going to pass out in the lift. I don't know what she's done to herself.'

'Well, let's find out, shall we?' soothed Penny. 'Now, Carole, if you sit here on this chair we ran rest your arm on the bunk. It's just the right height, see?'

'It hurts so much when I move it, Miss!' The eyes were beginning to swim again.

'I think it'll be easier if you lay it somewhere to support it, Carole.' Penny gently encouraged the girl to rest her forearm on the crisp white draw-sheet on the mattress top. The girl's face twisted with pain and there was a hiss of indrawn breath.

'Fine. Now I expect we can find a tissue,' said Penny, directing the other girl towards a dispenser on the wall. 'Have a blow—it always seems to help.'

With the two of them suitably diverted, she ran her fingers lightly down the arm. There was a swelling where the ulna and radius jointed on to the carpus.

'Can you move your wrist?' asked Penny gently.

'Oh no, Miss. It hurts too much.' Carole's eyes filled with alarm and she practically shrank back.

'Well we'd better *not* move it then,' smiled Penny reassuringly. 'Now, can you remember what happened exactly?'

'The filing cabinet was coming over on me. I forgot to close the bottom three drawers before I pulled out the top one and I just went to get out of the way, but I tripped over my feet and fell against a desk.'

'How? Palms down, you mean? Like this?' Penny mimed a fall against the bunk, hands outstretched.

'Yes, Nurse, just like that—but harder.'

'Thought so,' mused Penny. 'I think you might have cracked a bone in your wrist—the radius. Don't worry, it's very common. I can't be sure, but I think so. We'll have to take you for an X-ray at St Vincent's.'

Carole began to sniff again, but Penny had made her decision.

'Perhaps Mr Remington's secretary could ring personnel and see if we can get hold of a pool car. We've only to go across the river to the South Bank. Quarter of an hour's drive at this time of the afternoon. Meanwhile, we'll fix you up with an arm sling—it'll make things more comfortable.'

Within a few minutes, Penny was gently guiding her young charge, still distinctly wobbly, out through reception and into the back of an LTV car.

'Travelling in style today, Carole,' she smiled. 'You've even got a chauffeur.' She realised with a start that it was the same driver who had driven off with the arrogant Mr Welles just a short while ago. He could not have been going very far, she reflected.

'Company's keeping you busy this afternoon?' she ventured through the open glass partition.

'Not really, Sister. I've only had the lunch pick-up and set-down from Harley Street all day.'

The mention of Harley Street set more memory circuits vaguely connecting, but before Penny could enquire further, Carole was tugging at her sleeve.

'My Mum'll be worried,' she said.

'Don't worry, Carole. We can easily take care of that. I'll ring her from St Vincent's, once we've got you sorted out.' She smiled reassuringly and gave the girl's good hand a squeeze.

Within minutes, they were drawing up outside Accident and Emergency and Penny was helping Carole out and into the hospital. Even the preoccupations of the moment could not prevent a slight feeling of nostalgia as they passed through the entrance. It was, after all, the hospital where she had done her basic training, suffered her first pangs of homesickness in the nurses' home across the way—and then gradually flexed her wings as she passed her preliminaries and then her finals and made SRN, eventually settling down to a pleasant flat-sharing life with her friend Karen.

The feeling of being at home was completed as they made their way into A and E and walked straight into David Emerson.

'Good heavens, Penny. What are you doing here? Regained your senses at last and decided to come back to us?'

'No, not quite,' replied Penny, smiling in pleasure to see her flat-mate's fiancé. He was a friendly, outgoing person—a perfect match for Karen, who was also at St Vincent's running the children's ward with flair and affection. She had completely forgotten Karen's telling her that David was doing a spell as casualty officer.

'What's the trouble, then?' enquired David, who was eyeing Penny's young companion, taking in the sling and apprehensive expression.

'It looks to me as though we've got a Colles',' murmured Penny. 'I can't be sure, for there's hardly any misalignment. The hand certainly isn't carried back, so it isn't a severe break in the radius. But it was only a mild fall. I've a feeling that it's probably cracked, with the cartilage torn on the ulnar side. She's in some pain.'

'Well, young lady, I think it's preferential treatment for you. You're lucky to have come with an old St Vincent's staff member. We won't jump the queue exactly, for we're pretty quiet at this time of day. But we'll just sort of expedite matters.'

With his customary engaging grin, David led the way into a cubicle, made a swift examination which confirmed Penny's opinion and quickly organised them into X-ray to obtain a precise diagnosis. An hour later Carole was sitting back in A and E, her wrist securely plastered, the colour back in her cheeks and a second cup of tea chasing down the pain-killers which David had prescribed.

One telephone call from the reception desk communicated the nature of Carole's mishap to her mother, whose concern at the news was more than outweighed by gratitude at the efficiency with which Penny had dealt with things. A second call summoned another pool car to take Carole home, dropping Penny back at LTV first.

Back in the sick-bay, she smiled wryly down at her appointments diary as she tidied her desk and locked things up for the weekend. What had begun as a rather dull and empty afternoon had turned out quite surprisingly. She reflected that for a time there she had felt the old satisfaction of a challenge met and successfully dealt with. It had been good to go into St Vincent's again and to such a pleasant welcome. David and several others had given her no room for prevarication when she was asked if Clive was bringing her to the hospital's May Ball the following night. She realised she was really looking forward to it now, even though Clive had been a little lukewarm about going.

She sighed. It had been a whole twelve months ago that she had first met Clive, at last year's May Ball, and she had hoped that he would have been keener to go again this year. Their relationship had come a long way indeed from that first meeting and she lingered warmly on the love she felt for him, which she knew was reciprocated. He was a trainee television director at LTV and she had really fallen for his light-hearted manner and easy charm.

It was largely because of him that she had come to the company in the first place. The irregular hours which she had been working on men's surgical had not been helping their romance to flourish and he had promised her that she would enjoy the job at LTV.

She finished changing out of her uniform into the pleated skirt and jumper that she had travelled to work in that morning and, on a sudden resolve, picked up the phone to ring him. He usually worked late for, as he put it, one needed to maintain a 'presence' in the television industry. He was working on a short, twice-a-week children's programme but had hopes of bigger things soon.

'Clive Shaw speaking.'

'Oh Clive, it's Penny. I was just on my way off duty. I wondered what you were up to this evening.'

'Well actually, darling, I'm going to stick around. The powers that be are having a big pow-pow and there's definitely some news in the offing. I think little old yours truly might be in with a chance.'

'Oh Clive, how fabulous!' She paused. 'I've had quite an eventful afternoon, too.'

'Have you, darling? I'm really glad. What's been happening?'

'Well, we've had a Colles' fracture, that's a broken bone in the wrist. A girl in accounts. I've been over to St Vincent's and met all the old—'

'That's really great,' interrupted Clive. 'Look love, I think the meeting's breaking up. I've just seen Wheeler coming out of his office. He usually goes for a gin and tonic down in the hospitality suite bar about this time. I think I'll slope along there too, see if I can find out what's in the air. Why don't you come down as well?'

'Well no, I don't think so,' she hesitated. Despite being at LTV for nearly three months, she did not quite feel comfortable with all the television types. The conversation always seemed so specialised, with so much jargon, that she felt rather left out. It must be a little like that for Clive, when her friends were all talking shop, she realised. She resolved not to let that happen on the following night.

'I think I'll go home and have an early night,' she went on. 'Get some beauty sleep for tomorrow.'

'Tomorrow?' enquired Clive.

'Yes . . . the May Ball!' She waited for a response. 'But you hadn't forgotten, had you?'

'Oh, er, no.' He sounded rather uncertain.

'You do still want to go, Clive, don't you? I'm so looking forward to it.'

'Yes, of course, darling. It's just that my parents have been asking to meet you and I've half said we'd go down and stay tomorrow night. They've asked us to Sunday lunch and I thought we could—'

'Oh Clive, you *had* forgotten!'

'Well, I'm afraid it had slipped my mind, old thing,' he admitted.

There was an awkward silence. Penny twisted the telephone cord uncertainly, disappointed that he obviously did not want to go. But it was important that his parents wanted to meet her. And if he was about to hear some good news about his career, he might be planning all sorts of things. Her heart quickened. She had a sudden flash of inspiration.

'How about driving down to your parents' after the ball? We needn't stay till the end.'

'That's a great idea, Penny,' he exclaimed.

'You wouldn't be too tired?' she added hastily. 'Tenterden's quite a way.'

'No problem,' he announced. 'I'll pick you up at

seven-thirty. You can leave a weekend bag in the car while we're at the ball. I'll ring Mum this evening to say we'll be arriving late.'

'That's settled then,' said Penny with relief.

'Yes, well, must dash, darling. See you tomorrow. Bye.'

She replaced the receiver and closed up the sick-bay. She made her way to the lifts and out of Strand Tower, bidding a cheery farewell to George, her mind filled with a pleasant sense of anticipation. Karen, her flatmate, was already home when she arrived and the two girls spent a companionable half hour in the kitchen, gossiping about the week's happenings and preparing some supper. News of her visit to St Vincent's that afternoon had reached Karen, who relayed how all the old crowd were looking forward to seeing her again at the ball.

'And then down to his parents, eh?' laughed Karen. 'Do you think he's on the brink of popping the question?'

'Oh, heaven knows,' replied Penny. 'With Clive, it's impossible to pin him down. But I suppose he might be thinking about it.' She trailed off, staring into the middle distance.

'How fabulous. Who knows? We both might be wearing engagement rings in a little while. I mean it is what you want, Penny, isn't it?'

'Oh yes, Karen,' she replied. 'Definitely. I'd feel so much more settled. I know he loves me, and I'd stop fretting about whether I made a mistake leaving Vinnie's if I had wedding plans to make.'

'Well, let's keep our fingers crossed. Now then, I do believe that spaghetti's just about ready. You strain it and I'll get a couple of trays. There's a good film on the telly and we can eat it on our laps.'

The two girls spent a pleasant evening watching an old Ingrid Bergman film. Karen, a real romantic, was sniffing as it ended and blew her nose loudly. She was lucky to have good, down-to-earth David for a fiancé, reflected Penny. They were perfect for each other. David acted as a sort of sheet-anchor for Karen's emotions, while her fancy-free spirit stopped him from becoming too set in his ways. They would make a fine marriage. Perhaps it was soon to be that way with herself and Clive, she thought, feeling a slight tremor of nervousness at the thought of meeting his parents.

'Have you thought what you're going to wear tomorrow?' asked Karen suddenly.

'Heavens, no,' replied Penny. 'I really must go and sort that out now.' She paused at the door. 'I nearly bought a new dress this lunch-time. It was quite something.'

'Why didn't you?'

'Oh, I don't know. Wasn't in the right mood, I expect.'

'Why don't we go up to town tomorrow morning and you can try it on again? You might feel in the spirit of things more.'

'No, I'll have a look through my faithful old wardrobe, I think. I've bought quite a few new things this spring that nobody at St Vincent's will have seen.' Wishing Karen goodnight and telling her to leave the washing-up for her to do in the morning, she retired to her room.

In the end, she decided that her rose-coloured silk jump suit would be perfect for the Ball. It was also the right mixture of casual and formal in case they stayed to dinner with Clive's parents the next day. Her high-heeled silver sandals would complete the outfit. She would leave the selection of her other clothes for the trip until tomorrow. She hung up the jump suit to remind her to iron it first thing in the morning and started putting away her clothes from that day.

She picked up her court shoes to put in the wardrobe and her umbrella as well, returning it to its accustomed place in the corner. As she did so, she felt the roughness of the handle where the revolving doors had caught it and she felt a prickle of annoyance as she recalled the embarrassment of her encounter that lunch-time.

Later, she drifted off into a delicious sleep, her conscious mind sliding easily into oblivion. Her subconscious, however, remained hard at work, probing away at just where she had seen the striking features of Mr Justin Welles before.

CHAPTER TWO

'ARE YOU sure you don't want to come in our car?' called Karen from the hallway. Penny stuck her head out of the living-room to see her friend looking back anxiously for an answer. David was standing behind her, the front door held open.

'It's nearly eight o'clock now,' he said. 'Clive may have had a problem with the car. You don't want to miss any of the fun, Penny.'

'No, I'll wait,' said Penny. 'If he has had a problem with the car, he'll ring here. Thanks anyway. You two go on ahead. We'll catch you up. The ball never really gets going until nine or ten anyway.'

'All right then, if you're sure. See you later.' The front door clicked shut and Penny walked over to the window to look down on the street below. She watched Karen and David drive off and scanned the end of the road for Clive. Seeing no sign of him, she sat down in an armchair and began idly flicking through a magazine.

She could find nothing absorbing in it but, as was often her habit, turned to the end pages to the advice columns. She did this more out of professional interest than for light relief, for she believed such features provided a real social benefit. A lot of people found it much easier to address a question by mail to a distant figure than to discuss their symptoms personally, especially if they were young or easily embarrassed. And by and large they received well-considered and responsible advice.

This particular magazine, *Eve*, ran an extremely good advice column, for which the contributors were a panel, consisting of a lawyer, sociologist, accountant and doctor. She turned to the medical section.

Suddenly, there before her was the last link to complete the memory circuits in her mind. Staring back at her from the page was Dr Justin Welles, the medical member of the advice panel. It was a flattering photograph and he certainly looked mellower than the arrogant version she had met the previous lunch-time. There was no mistaking the strangely intense quality of the gaze or the classic line of the jaw, however. No hint of a smile was discernible in his expression and the mouth was set in a serious, hard line. This, however, did not prevent a certain sympathy emanating from his face—as befitted the magazine role he was obviously playing.

She felt a mild sense of disquiet, thinking back to their encounter, but was relieved that her memory had not been playing tricks. She must have flicked through this section of the magazine many times in the past and become aware of his face and name at a subconscious level, but it wasn't sufficiently well-remembered to be able to recall it openly. It was, after all, a very small photograph which appeared on the page, only just bigger than passport size. At least the nagging familiarity about him which had been troubling her was now explained.

She resumed her study of the column, interested to see what manner he adopted when responding to readers' letters. She found him to be a lucid writer, with a reassuring streak of common sense and with absolutely no hint of talking down. A pity he couldn't find the same qualities in his dealings with people face to face, she reflected.

Her thoughts were interrupted by the doorbell and she was startled. Anticipation of the ball and Clive's arrival had totally left her mind for the moment.

She jumped up and, pausing only to collect her mac and the overnight bag she had packed, ran to the front door.

'Sorry I'm late, darling. Completely misjudged things. Is that your weekend bag? Here, let me take it.' He leaned forward and gave her a perfunctory peck on the cheek and turned back to the stairs, taking the bag from her.

She closed the door behind her and followed him down, slightly disappointed that he had not made any approving comments about her outfit. He always said he preferred her with her hair down, but somehow the more formal style of the chignon which she had decided upon seemed to match the silk jump suit much better. She felt a slight pang of doubt about this, however, for in comparison to Clive she seemed rather overdressed. He was wearing his chocolate brown sports coat and fawn slacks with his suede shoes. Most of the men would be more formal, she thought. Not dinner jackets of course, but a fair sprinkling of suits. Never mind, she sighed. At least they were going to make it—and not too late after all.

Clive seemed to sense her disappointment that they had missed the first hour and negotiated the drive from her Fulham flat to the South Bank Hotel, the venue for the ball, with a great deal of panache—some of it a little unnecessary, she felt. But the Golf GTI had been a twenty-fifth birthday present from his parents and she knew he enjoyed its sporty performance.

Things were in full swing when they arrived. The music was provided by a really lively and well compèred disco, which managed to provide exactly the right mixture of easy, melodious music for the more mature staff, as well as the infectious, body-driving modern rhythms which Penny loved.

Within a very short space of time she was dragged away from Clive by a succession of partners, all of them friends and colleagues from her days at the hospital. There was much interest in how she was getting on at LTV, but conversation was slightly inhibited by the music. They had arrived in the midst of an up-tempo spell and there was little opportunity for any talk other than the usual pleasantries. It was good to renew old acquaintances though, and within a very short space of time she was enjoying herself immensely.

She caught a glimpse of Clive standing at the edge of the dance floor, a drink in his hand. Concerned that she was neglecting him, she made her way over. It was a warm night for the first of May and she could feel the colour in her cheeks from the rock and roll number she had just danced.

'Fancy a drink, then?' he asked.

'Not just yet, thank you, darling,' she replied, preferring the more natural stimulation of the music. 'Actually, a breath of fresh air would be nice. I think that door leads to a terrace overlooking the river. Unless you'd like to dance, of course?'

'No. It's much too warm for that,' he answered and turning, led the way outside.

It was cooler out here and there was a pleasant breeze blowing off the Thames. The terrace was not empty, however, for several couples were taking advantage of the shadows to dance closely together, swaying gently to the dreamy music that was being played. They made their way over to the balcony and looked out at the London skyline.

On their left were the Festival Hall and the National Theatre—and then the broad sweep of Victoria Embankment opposite, down-river to Blackfriars and the City. Many of the buildings were floodlit, their reflections clearly visible in the smooth-flowing river. In the background she could make out the dome of St Paul's, its cross clearly visible in a web of spotlights. A pleasure-boat was moving slowly up the tideway and she caught a hint of music floating up on the breeze, its sound mixing strangely with the strains from their own party.

'This must be one of the nicest places from which to look at London's skyline,' she said, slipping an affectionate arm through Clive's and leaning her head against his shoulder.

'I suppose it is,' he murmured vaguely.

'And a view which brings back memories of St Vincent's, I expect,' added a third voice and she realised that the couple next to them along the balcony consisted of Karen and David.

'Hallo, you two!' she cried. 'Are you enjoying yourselves?' Greetings were exchanged and Clive and David shook hands.

'Decided to come back yet, Penny?' asked David chidingly. She felt Clive stiffen.

'Come back?' he demanded. 'Come back where?'

'Oh, David's not serious,' reassured Penny. 'They keep trying to persuade me to come back to Vinnie's.'

'What on earth for?'

She paused for a moment, feeling a little resentful at the dismissive note in Clive's voice.

'Well, it's not all that unthinkable, Clive. I was very happy here and I felt I was learning all the time. LTV's very nice and everything, but . . .'

'Far more exciting, you mean. It was all bedpans and autoclaves when I first met you. You couldn't wait to get away.'

'That's not really true, Clive,' she replied quickly. Karen and David were maintaining a tactful, if slightly embarrassed, silence. 'It was the hours I was working that were difficult. We never seemed able to coincide with each other. Especially when I was doing splits.'

'Yes, that was absolutely impossible. Anyway, who's for another drink? Karen? David?'

'We're OK actually, thanks, Clive,' replied David.

'Well, this is a cheap round. What about you, Penny?'

'An orange juice would be lovely, Clive. With lots of ice, please.'

'Am I the only one in a party mood, then? Oh well, so be it.' He disappeared off through the balcony doors in the direction of the bar.

'Are you really missing St Vincent's, Penny?' asked Karen.

'Well, to tell you the truth, I am a bit. It's great at LTV—the hours are easier and everything—and it's nice to be able to see Clive more often, of course, but well . . .' she trailed off.

'It's not like running a ward.' David finished the sentence for her.

'Yes,' she said. 'That's it exactly. It's all right if I get an emergency or if I'm needed to do something that's important. Or just if I was kept a little busier. There was never a minute to yourself in men's surgical and, well, I do miss it.'

She would have added that she missed all the staff at St Vincent's even more, that she felt so isolated in her efficient little sick-bay in Strand Tower, that tonight's friendly company was making her feel quite nostalgic, but for a second she wasn't sure she could trust her voice and the sudden lump in her throat.

She was spared further comment by the arrival of one of David's colleagues who laughingly insisted on whirling Karen away, claiming that she had promised him a dance to the first Beatles' number that was played and that this was probably the last ball where David would allow her the freedom of being a single woman. Penny smilingly agreed to follow suit and partner David whilst Clive was still at the bar.

It was an unexpectedly long medley and when she excused herself and went back to look for Clive, she was surprised to find that he was still absent. She eventually tracked him down in the bar itself, where she found him sitting on a stool, deep in conversation with a tall, lanky individual whom she recognised but could not quite place.

'You remember Nigel, don't you, Penelope?' He put an arm round her waist and pulled her a little roughly to him. 'It was Nigel who brought us together in the first place, wasn't it?' Penny looked puzzled. 'Oh, you remember, darling! I came as his guest last year.'

'Oh yes, of course,' she exclaimed. 'Hallo, Nigel, how are you? Didn't you leave St Vincent's last Christmas?'

'That's right, Penny. I never really was going to make

it in medicine. Went into the old man's property business. He made me an offer I couldn't refuse, eh?'

She smiled in acknowledgement and rather hesitantly accepted the stool which Nigel pushed towards her.

She realised that her two companions were anxious to catch up with each other's news and she tolerantly sat and sipped her orange juice, listening to their banter. She became a little concerned, however, to see that there were already two empty glasses on the bar where they sat and when Clive suggested a third round, she felt that his voice was becoming just a little too uninhibited.

'Clive, do you really think you should? I mean, it's a long drive to Tenterden and you don't want to get stopped or anything. And alcohol's deceptive. You think you're all right, but . . .'

'I'm perfectly all right, Penelope,' he replied, but she insisted.

'You've already got one endorsement for speeding,' she reminded him.

'Yes,' he said reluctantly. He looked at Nigel. 'I suppose Sister's right, Nige. You can tell she's used to ordering patients about, can't you? It's a pity. I was just beginning to enjoy myself.'

On a sudden impulse, Penny went on, 'I'd offer to drive for you, but I'm not all that sure of your car on a really long journey.' She hesitated. 'Why don't you ring your parents and say we've changed our plans and are coming down in the morning? I'm sure your mother won't mind. We'd have been terribly late anyway. Then you can enjoy yourself. I'm sure I can manage to drive the car to your flat. That's just a short distance.'

He frowned, but then grudgingly agreed and went off to telephone. She was glad that her voice of reason had prevailed, for she remembered that he had also had a drink when they first arrived.

'That's all fixed then,' he announced, as he negotiated his way back to them through the press of people round the bar. 'Now we can really catch up with each other, Nigel.'

And catch up they really had, thought Penny ruefully as she woke up the next morning. Sometimes Clive really was like an overgrown schoolboy. By the time the last dance came and he had gallantly, but a little boisterously, taken to the floor with her, she was very thankful she had persuaded him against the journey. She had managed to drive his car quite well, despite never having done so before—and despite not being used to a car for some time herself. She had learned to drive as soon as she was seventeen, with her father's encouragement, but apart from trying to run an ancient and soon-pensioned-off Morris, she had never really had her own transport.

Poor Clive would very likely have quite a hangover, she thought, raising her head to listen intently for any sounds from the next room. He had grudgingly insisted that she take the bedroom whilst he slept in a sleeping-bag on the settee in the living-room. She had gladly accepted and been a little relieved to retire from his goodnight kiss, which had been rather insistent. They were practically engaged she knew, but she wanted the first night they slept together to be absolutely perfect—and not the casual aftermath of a rather uninhibited evening.

She slid quietly out of bed and put her dressing-gown on over her nightie. She would seek out some paracetamol from the bathroom and make him a cup of tea. She picked up her watch from the bedside table. Heavens, it was nine-thirty! They certainly must arrive in respectable time for lunch on her first visit to his parents. She flew into the kitchen to put on the kettle, tactfully rattling the lid in order to at least start Clive on a return to consciousness.

By the time she came back, he was stirring. He pulled himself up on one elbow as she put the tea down by his side and gently rattled the paracetamol.

'Sister Shepherd prescribes a nice hot cup of tea and two analgesics,' she announced softly. He groaned and held a hand to the back of his neck.

'Exactly,' she observed. 'It's coming up to ten o'clock and I'm just going to jump in the bath, if that's all right. Then you can have the bathroom to yourself while I get dressed. We really shouldn't be late at your parents'— especially after not turning up last night.'

There was a further groan which she assumed to be one of assent and she retired to the bathroom, pausing only to collect her own mug of tea on the way.

An hour later found them on the road to Tenterden. Clive was still distinctly fragile but the orange juice, coffee and toast which she had prepared had obviously produced some beneficial effects. She sat back in her seat, enjoying the drive down through the spring countryside. Everywhere was the flutter of new leaves and she gaily tried to draw Clive's attention to the lambs she could see frisking about in the fields, but he was concentrating on his driving.

She knew that his parents lived in a beautifully converted eighteenth-century farmhouse and she sat forward in interest as they turned off the main road on the outskirts of the town and up a short driveway. She had dressed with care, deciding in the end on a smart but comfortable blue jersey dress, with a neat leather belt encircling her trim waist. She wondered for the hundredth time that morning what their hosts would make of her.

She was certainly not prepared for the slightly distant manner in which she was greeted, particularly by Clive's mother. For a moment she almost sensed an attitude of disapproval in the cool handshake. They were led into a large lounge, with sliding glass doors looking out over a terraced garden. A beautiful grand piano stood in the corner.

'Oh, you're a musical family,' she exclaimed. 'Which one of you plays? Is it you, Mrs Shaw?'

'No, dear. We bought it when Clive was having lessons, but he had to give it up when he was doing his 'O' levels. Didn't you, dear?' Mrs Shaw smiled at her son, a little indulgently, Penny thought.

'When he discovered girls, you mean,' interrupted Clive's father, taking Penny's arm and winking. He steered her over to a cocktail cabinet.

'Well, I'm going to have a little tipple before lunch. What about you, Penelope? What's your poison?'

She asked for a medium sherry and settled back into an armchair, sipping her drink. Clive and his mother were ensconced on the long settee and she found herself talking with Mr Shaw. Or rather he did most of the talking. He was a keen golfer and usually played on Sunday morning. In fact, she gained the impression that he would have preferred to be on the links *that* morning rather than entertaining his son's girlfriend, but she banished this rather disloyal thought and listened politely. Eventually, lunch was served and they went through to the dining room.

'I expect I've been monopolising Clive,' said Mrs Shaw to Penny as she led the way. 'We can have a nice little chat after lunch. I always like to get to know Clive's girlfriends.'

There was indeed an opportunity for a 'little chat' after lunch, for Clive and his father had hardly settled back after coffee before their eyelids drooped and they were both fast asleep.

Penny, who had managed to resist Mr Shaw's generosity with the wine, found herself wide awake. She eagerly agreed when Mrs Shaw asked if she would like to see over the house. They started with Clive's old room. 'I expect you'd like to see it,' his mother had said.

It was a pleasant room, kept beautifully clean despite the plethora of boyhood possessions—model aeroplanes, a cricket bat, posters, a stamp collection and so forth—which still filled it.

'I try and keep it ready for him in case he ever needs it,' said Mrs Shaw. 'He used to come home most weekends, bring his washing for me to do. Mind you, we don't see so much of him these days.' There was a rather uncomfortable silence and Penny almost imagined that she detected a note of resentment.

'What about his elder sister? Do you see much of her?'

'Oh no,' said Mrs Shaw. 'Even though she's only in the next county. Married into a farming family, you know. Her father and I were very against it, but she always was an obstinate girl. She's regretting it now, mind you. That sort of life's just slave labour. If she's not actually working outside on the farm itself, she's trapped in the kitchen. Morning to night.'

'It needn't be like that,' protested Penny, unable to conceal the defensive reaction she felt. 'My father is a farmer, actually,' she added. There was a pause.

'Oh, really?'

This time, Penny was certain she could hear a note of disapproval and she hurriedly changed the subject and asked to see the garden. Mrs Shaw agreed, but in a rather unenthusiastic manner, explaining that most of it was done by a man who came in two or three times a week.

As they strolled around the well-ordered and some-what uninspired beds and borders, Penny concluded that she was not really enjoying this visit at all. The chief subject of Clive's mother's conversation seemed to be Clive, and any effort she made to enquire about Penny's background seemed more like interrogation than interest. In fact, Penny had an overwhelming impression that she was being vetted—and compared to some mysterious set of standards it would be impossible to measure up to. Gradually her normally polite and friendly conversation lapsed into silence, punctuated by the very minimum of monosyllabic responses to what Mrs Shaw was saying.

It was difficult to contain the relief she felt when Clive suggested they should return to London after a cup of tea had revived him from his post-prandial nap.

'Yes dear, you're looking very tired. I expect you need an early night,' fussed Mrs Shaw—and then glanced at Penny, almost as if she were in some way the cause of Clive's lack of sleep.

Inwardly fuming, she replied that she, too, needed to be back in London, almost hoping that the animosity in her voice would be noticed. But of course it was not.

'What did you think of them?' asked Clive breezily as they drove back homewards. Penny was nonplussed and searched for some non-committal reply.

'They have a beautiful house,' she said eventually. And then added, 'Your mother's very fond of you, isn't she?'

'Oh yes,' he said happily. 'Goes on a bit, though.' He laughed. 'I think she thinks I'm always about to rush off and get married. Keeps saying I must get my career going first. But she needn't worry, need she?'

Penny looked across at him, a sinking feeling inside her. 'About your career, you mean?' she said.

'No. I mean . . .' He looked up and fiddled with the rear-view mirror in an oddly embarrassed sort of manner. 'That is, about getting married.' He paused but she made no attempt to break the silence. 'I mean, nobody wants to get married too young these days, do they? There's no need. And anyway, you've got to live a little first. Have fun. Meet plenty of people.'

The silence continued and he grew even more hesitant.

'Well, you know what I mean, darling. You agree with that, I know. And you've got your career, too. You're certainly not the sort of girl who'd want to rush into anything, are you?' He snatched a sideways glance at her. Unable to reply, she shook her head dumbly.

The rest of the journey passed interminably slowly, her only concern being how she could end this thoroughly horrid trip the minute she got back to her flat. She need not have worried, however, for as they drew up he peered at himself in the mirror and announced that yes, he was looking a bit tired and yes, she probably would like a quiet evening as well. Seizing her opportunity, she quickly grabbed her weekend case from the back seat and jumped out of the car, pausing only for the briefest peck on the cheek before fleeing up the steps and through the front door.

In her room, she sat on her bed and stared disconsolately into space. It was the humiliation that hurt most. She had really been looking forward to meeting Clive's parents. She imagined that he would have told them something about her in advance, but she had been received as just another one of his girlfriends. Had she really been imagining that the visit was going to be a prelude to a proposal? The conversation in the car had indicated that marriage was the last thing on his mind. She lay back on the bed, pillowing her head on her hands. The visit really had been a bit of a strain, she told herself—and she had probably been a little overwrought, probably got everything out of proportion.

The flat was empty and she remembered that Karen had been doing an early shift, about which she had been good-naturedly complaining the night before. Penny swung her legs off the bed. It was pointless mooning about like this, she told herself as she slipped out of her dress and hung it up. Perhaps Clive was just wary of getting tied down. No different to any other man. Perhaps she was smothering him a little. After all, she did have rather a lot of time without enough to really occupy her mind at work. That would certainly make her place far too much emphasis on their relationship. He loved her in his own fashion, she knew, and she never doubted that he was faithful to her. That was it—they were probably taking each other too much for granted. The best thing was to make some changes in her own life. That would bring some freshness to their relationship.

The sound of Karen's key in the door disturbed this reverie and she pulled on her jeans and a sweater, filled with new resolve.

'Hi,' she called through her open bedroom door.

'Hi, yourself,' came the reply and a rather jaded Karen appeared, leaning wearily against the door jamb. 'How was your day?'

'All right,' replied Penny hurriedly. 'How was yours?'

'A bit overshadowed by the night before,' said Karen ruefully.

'Cup of tea?' enquired Penny sympathetically.

'Fabulous.'

'Go and get changed then, and I'll put the kettle on. And I'll do the supper later.'

'You're a friend indeed,' said Karen gratefully.

Penny sped into the kitchen, feeling much better, her mind filled with the positiveness of the decision she had made a few minutes earlier. She could not resist telling Karen what she intended to do, as they sat in their sitting-room later that evening.

'I've decided to leave LTV,' she announced.

'Have you, Penny?' Karen was surprised. 'But what about Clive? Won't he mind?'

'I've decided I've got things rather out of proportion,' said Penny.

'Is it not going very well between you, then?'

'Well, it's not that exactly. It's just that I think it's better if we each have our own lives outside the relationship. Well, you know what I mean. I think we've got a bit obsessed with each other.'

'Yes, I do know what you mean. David and I certainly shan't both stay on at St Vincent's together once we're married. And it's not because we're going to start a family straight away either. It's better for David's career to move on and it'll mean we'll have news for each other during off-duty. Not just going over the same old hospital gossip we've both heard during the day.'

They subsided into a companionable silence.

'Are you going to come back to St Vincent's?' asked Karen suddenly.

'I don't know,' said Penny slowly. 'I think I really want to turn over a whole new leaf. Find something really different.' She paused and then went on firmly, 'I shall sleep on it, but I'm pretty sure I shall start job-hunting tomorrow. At least have a look to see what's going.'

Her intentions in this direction were somewhat frustrated, for apart from a brief skim through *Nursing Mirror* during her coffee-break, she was kept busy for a change—right through the next morning. She was pleased to see that young Carole was back at work, the memory of Friday's unpleasant experience beginning to recede. Much to Carole's embarrassment, her boyfriend had insisted on drawing a large heart, suitably initialled, on her plaster cast and the rest of the accounts department had rapidly followed his lead with other embellishments.

'I don't think there's a square centimetre of plaster free from autographs,' observed Penny laughingly. 'But it's comfortable enough, is it?'

'It still hurts, Sister, but nothing like it was on Friday. It's a good job it's my left arm.'

'When do they want to see you again at St Vincent's?'

'Two weeks today.'

'Good. Right then. Come down and see me if you're at all concerned about anything, won't you?'

When she came back from lunch she settled down at

her desk to scan the situations vacant column in the nursing journals, but had barely started reading when the phone rang.

'Penny, it's me, Clive. Are you busy this afternoon?'

She was slightly taken aback. 'Well, I don't know, Clive. What is it?'

'It's all very exciting. You know I said there was something brewing up on Friday? Well, I've just had lunch with Wheeler and he wants me to work on a new documentary series that LTV are going to put out in the autumn. He says I'm to be studio director.'

'That's really good, Clive. I'm very pleased for you.' She realised, to her slight surprise, that her voice sounded rather cool, but Clive did not seem to be aware of it.

'Anyway, there are to be three pilot shows to see how it goes and then we'll probably go out on air with six. A weekly series. If it's a success there'll be another series in the spring.'

'What are the programmes going to be about?'

'Well, that's the whole point. You can really help me. It's going to be a medical series. Probably called *Life Lines*. I've talked to Wheeler about you and he thinks it's a good idea.'

'Clive, just *what* is a good idea? I don't understand!'

'For you to work on the programme, of course. We need a sort of PA. Somebody who has some real medical knowledge, to help the researchers. I thought we might as well make use of—'

'But Clive, I know nothing about television!'

'That doesn't matter at all. You don't need to know anything about television. We've got hordes of technicians to take care of all the backroom stuff. No, it's help with the programme-making that Wheeler wants. He wants a sort of interpreter to help him and the producer with all the medical jargon, work with the script-writers and so forth.'

'I see,' said Penny uncertainly. 'But I've still got my job here to do.'

'Wheeler says that's no problem at all. Most of the time you'll still be in Strand Tower, so you'll be on the premises if you're needed suddenly. And if you're going to be out of the building for any period, you can hire an agency nurse.'

Despite herself, she felt a tremor of excitement. Certainly, what Clive was saying seemed possible, but her mind was buzzing with questions. She realised Clive was hanging on, waiting for some reaction.

'Well, what do you say, Penny? It would do me so much good to be the one who found the solution to the problem. And working on the series will really clinch my career.'

'Yes, Clive, I can see that.' A thought crossed her mind that just a minute ago she had been thinking very hard about *her* career—but the words did not come. Working on a medical programme would be a fascinating project, though. It could be just what she needed to get out of the rut she was in.

'What exactly will I be doing, Clive?' she asked, trying to sound non-committal.

'Haven't time to go into it all now. That's what all the rush is about. If we're going to make the autumn schedules, we need to have a first pre-production conference this afternoon. It's the only chance we're going to get to meet the presenter for the series. He flies out to Switzerland tomorrow—and next week, when he's back, is too late. Part of your job will be to liaise with him, so it's important you meet him.'

'Who is he?'

'Oh, some leading Harley Street man. He's a complete unknown as a television personality, but I believe he has some experience in journalism. Hang on, I've written his name down somewhere . . . Justin somebody. I'll just put the phone down while I look.'

She could hear him rustling through papers. She was far more aware of the thudding of her heart, however, for she was almost sure she knew what the surname was going to be.

A seemingly interminable period of time passed before she heard the clatter as he picked up the receiver again.

'Here it is—*Welles*, that's it. Justin Welles.'

She realised she had been holding her breath and let it out in a rush.

'I can tell Wheeler you'll be at the pre-production meeting then, can I? It's in conference suite B on the seventh floor. Four-thirty.'

Penny took another deep breath and made her decision.

'Yes, Clive, you can tell Mr Wheeler I'll be there.'

CHAPTER THREE

SHE REPLACED the receiver and realised she was still
staring at the appointments column in *Nursing Mirror*.
Minutes before, she had been studying it intently, her
mind made up to leave LTV. Now she was about to get
involved in heaven knew what instead.

Despite Clive's airy dismissal of her concerns, she felt
a mild flutter of trepidation at the thought of this afternoon's conference. She found most television types,
other than Clive of course, rather overpowering—and
there was also the supercilious Dr Welles to be reckoned
with. She determined she was not going to let him get the
better of her in the coming meeting. Nevertheless, she
knew she would feel very much out of her depth in a
discussion about the more complex aspects of television
production, particularly if everybody started using all
that incomprehensible jargon.

It suddenly struck her that it was quite possible the lofty
Dr Welles would have a similar difficulty. How had Clive
described him? *A complete unknown as far as television
was concerned*—that was it. He would be no better
equipped than she for all the technical details.

She looked at her watch. Three o'clock, almost. She
had an hour or so before the meeting. She would fill in
the time by bringing her Kardex record system up to date
with last week's activities. She set to, but found her mind
wandering.

Should she go to the meeting in her uniform? It was

hardly a uniform in the sense of the sister's blue ward dress and starched cap which she used to wear at St Vincent's. At LTV she favoured a very straightforward affair in white. Even so, it did seem a little excessive to wear it to the meeting. It would give her a sense of identity, admittedly, but since she was really attending in her professional capacity, it did not seem appropriate. In fact, she was very uncertain as to precisely in what capacity she *was* attending. She decided that it would be best to change back into the skirt and jacket she had worn to work that morning. Together with her plain court shoes and white blouse it would give her a businesslike air which would help her confidence.

So it was that she found herself taking the lift to the seventh floor a short time later, notebook and pencil in hand and very unsure of herself. Up here on the conference floor it was all luxurious fitted carpets, indoor plants and air conditioning. She followed a sign down a corridor towards the panelled door of conference suite B. She hesitated before it and gave a tap on its polished wooden surface. She could hear a buzz of conversation from inside but no invitation to enter. Feeling a little foolish, she turned the handle and diffidently stuck her head round the door. There was a group of people standing at one end of a long conference table, deep in discussion over some sort of plan laid out before them. Nobody looked up at her and she stepped into the room and stood there awkwardly, uncertain as to whether she was even in the right place.

A rather portly man, with grey-streaked dark hair suddenly noticed her and gave her a quizzical look. She recognised him as Jeremy Wheeler, head of LTV documentaries. She stepped forward determinedly.

'I'm Sister Shepherd,' she said, with a great deal more confidence than she felt. The puzzled expression on Mr Wheeler's face cleared, to be replaced by a warm smile.

'Ah yes, Sister, of course,' he said. 'Young Shaw mentioned you. You're going to give us some help with *Life Lines*, aren't you? Excellent. Excellent.' He came over and shook her hand. 'I'm Jeremy Wheeler. But let me introduce you to the people who really do the work.'

He took her arm and steered her over to the group round the table. She was introduced to a rather tense, nervously energetic type of person called Angus Murray, who turned out to be the producer, plus several other people who were apparently to do with script-writing, programme research and set design. Of Clive—or indeed Dr Justin Welles—there was no sign as yet.

'In fact, Sister,' went on Jeremy Wheeler, 'we are just taking a look at the first ideas for the studio set now. We're trying to get the feel of a consultant's room in a modern hospital. Perhaps you could take a look at it and tell us what you think.'

The group at the end of the table made way for her and she found herself staring down at an extremely compli-cated sort of plan, all drawn on paper covered with squares, like graph paper, with areas hatched in, lines forming strange shapes and all over it, an indecipherable scrawl. She shook her head in dismay.

'I'm afraid I don't . . .' she faltered.

'It's a sort of ground-plan for the set.' The man who had been introduced as the designer came to her rescue. 'It looks far more confusing than it is, really. It's just a first scribble so that we can start working on the camera angles and provide a background against which the script-writers can work.'

'Oh, I see,' answered Penny, slightly relieved to see a tray of tea being brought in and removing her from the focus of attention. She bent over the plan and studied it.

'These are what we call flats,' went on the designer, pointing with a felt pen. 'Artificial walls,' he explained hurriedly as he saw the mystified look in her eye. 'One wall is missing from the room, so that the cameras can see in.'

'Oh, now I see . . .' The lines and scrawls began to take shape. She realised that Angus Murray, the producer, was standing at her side, holding out a cup of tea for her. She took it with a smile of thanks.

'The idea is for Dr Welles to sit in on an interview between the consultant and his patient, so that he can explain to the viewers what's going on. We're going to use real consultants and real patients and obviously they're not used to talking with the public. That's Dr Welles' job. Also, he's the link-man for the whole series.'

'I see,' said Penny.

'We thought we'd sit him here, in the foreground, to one side of the consultant's desk, with the patient here—'

'Oh, but I don't think the consultant would have a desk between himself and the patient,' said Penny, looking down at the set design again. 'Mostly these days, desks are against walls, with the consultant able to turn sideways to talk to his patient. It's far less of a barrier than to have him actually behind a desk. It helps patients relax more.'

'Yes, indeed.' The designer was pulling at his chin. 'I see what you mean. Actually, that makes the whole set much simpler. We can put Dr Welles here and the desk here, turn this round here . . .' He became lost in thought, felt pen sketching furiously. He suddenly looked back up at her and grinned. 'Well, Sister, it's going to be great having you around. You've already made my job a sight easier just with that one observation.'

Penny flushed with pleasure, her confidence soaring. At that moment, the door flew open to the accompaniment of a fit of giggles and a girl appeared, her cheeks somewhat flushed, precariously balancing a pile of folders and what looked like videotapes. Clive was also visible, holding the door open for her.

'Ah, there you are, Samantha,' boomed Mr Wheeler. 'And you too, Clive. Nice of you to come along,' he added ironically.

'Sorry we're late, Jeremy,' said Clive. 'Sam was having a bit of trouble with the photocopier. I gave her a hand.' There was a further giggle from the girl, who had started laying out the folders on the long conference table. Clive caught sight of Penny and came over.

'Ah, there you are,' he said. 'Been introduced to everyone?'

'Yes, she has,' interposed Angus Murray, the producer. 'In fact, she's already made a very helpful suggestion.'

For a second Penny almost thought she saw a hint of annoyance in Clive's eyes, but it was swiftly gone, if it had been there at all.

'That's great,' he said. 'I knew you'd agree that having her on the series was one of my better ideas.' He seemed to be looking around to everybody for approval, not unlike a small boy, she felt—but nobody seemed to be paying much attention.

'It rather looks as though Dr Welles has been delayed,' announced Jeremy Wheeler. 'He did say that might happen, he's a busy man. I think we might as well make a start. At least we can all be reading through the programme outline. Please take a seat everyone.'

Penny sat down between the designer and one of the script-writers. Jeremy Wheeler took the head of the table with Angus on his right. An empty chair was left on his other side. Clive and the Samantha girl sat opposite her. He leaned forward.

'Sam's going to be my assistant on the series,' he explained and Penny acknowledged the girl's greeting. She was slightly surprised at this information, for she had assumed that Samantha was only a junior secretary. She hardly seemed out of her teens.

'Well, ladies and gentlemen, let's start with the programme concept,' continued Jeremy Wheeler. 'If you'd all like to refresh your memories as to the intentions for the series—or in your case, Sister Shepherd, discover what it's all about—' he smiled, 'you'll find it all written up in the blue folder.'

Clive picked up the folder in front of him and indicated that she should do the same. It seemed that *Life Lines* was to be a series of programmes designed to track a case from the first diagnosable symptoms, right through to treatment and a successful outcome. The patient would be seen discussing his or her problem at referral stage with a consultant—this was presumably to take place in the set she had been looking at—and then the programme would move to the hospital concerned, watch the surgery in theatre, then the recovery stage from high dependency through to low, and finally the return to normal life.

There would inevitably be a great deal of filming on

location, away from the studio, she realised, some of it quite complex. She felt a surge of interest as the scope of the series was described. She looked down the list of subjects under the heading Proposed Programme Content—osteo-arthritis with arthroplasty treatment, cholecystectomy, eye conditions, ENT surgery, possibly involving micro-surgery, and then, as the series developed, open-heart surgery and possibly high-tech carcinoma treatment, although the difficulties and emotional aspects attaching to these conditions were clearly acknowledged.

Penny's—and everybody else's—absorption in the document was interrupted as the conference-room door opened with a flourish and she found herself again looking up at the tall figure of Dr Justin Welles.

Jeremy Wheeler jumped up and went to greet him, hand extended.

'Justin!' he said. 'Good to see you. Come and join us.'

'I'm sorry I'm late, Jeremy. My three-thirty appointment took longer than I anticipated.' The voice was cultured, the tone courteous and measured. He moved towards the vacant chair and looked around the meeting with interest, his eyes passing along the line of faces, taking in Penny's, passing on—then suddenly pausing and returning to her. She felt the same disquiet again as they held her gaze. She had a strong desire to swallow, but somehow it did not quite come off. It was only a momentary second glance he gave her but she was sure she saw recognition flicker in the steel-blue depths and a sardonic smile tug at the corner of the hard mouth.

'Let me introduce everybody,' went on Jeremy Wheeler, leading him around the table. 'Angus Murray, who's going to be producing the series, then Tim

O'Driscoll, the designer. Penny Shepherd, who's going to be—'

'I think we might have bumped into each other before,' he observed and she felt her hand being taken in a light but firm grasp.

'Yes, I—' she started, but he had moved on round the table, making jokes with the script-writers about their having to buy a medical dictionary before they could handle all the complicated terminology. He gave Clive and the Samantha girl the briefest of handshakes and then took the empty chair next to Wheeler, lifting an elegant leather brief-case up on to the table and clicking back the locks with a lean, long-fingered hand. They were surgeon's fingers, finely formed and sensitive, but suggesting an innate strength.

'Samantha, dear, perhaps you could pour Dr Welles some tea and we'll get started,' said Wheeler. 'We've just been looking through the programme outline, Justin—ah, I see you've brought your copy. It's more or less what we discussed at lunch last Friday.'

Dr Welles inclined his head in a curt nod, withdrew one of the blue folders from his case and snapped shut the locks.

'Yes, I've been reading through it in the car on the way over. There are a few things which concern me, Jeremy, but I think as a feasibility statement it's fine.' He opened the report and, slipping a hand inside the elegant dove-grey suit jacket he was wearing, withdrew a slim silver pen from an inside pocket. He leant to one side to deposit his brief-case on the floor by his chair, narrowly missing the cup of tea which Samantha had been rather incautiously about to place at his elbow. She stepped back and everybody held their breath as the cup rattled precariously in its saucer, but the girl managed to retrieve the situation.

'Oh, Dr Welles, I'm sorry! I nearly spilt your tea down your—'

'Quite.' His upward glance stilled her and he leaned exaggeratedly to one side to enable her to place the tea safely on the table. Samantha returned to her seat, exchanging a rather foolish grin with Clive. For a second, Penny really thought the girl was going to giggle again. The doctor, meanwhile, was completely unruffled and was turning the pages of the report.

'I've made a note or two. Shall I air my thoughts first?'

'By all means, Justin,' answered Angus Murray, leaning forward.

'Well, firstly, I take it that our number one objective is to inform and educate?' Receiving a nod of assent from Angus Murray, he went on, 'And often the best way of doing that is to entertain?'

'A very good television principle, Justin,' observed Wheeler. 'Do go on.'

'Right. In that case, I suggest we place the intended cases we are going to study in ascending order of difficulty and seriousness. That way, we'll start with the more common problems and therefore those with the widest public interest. This will ensure that we achieve a good audience right from the outset. Then, as things develop and we're confident that the format works, we can add the more advanced cases.' He looked around the table for a reaction, but such was the shrewdness of his thoughts and the fluent and articulate manner in which he expressed them, that there was really no need for an answer.

'Yes, it's always a good thing to go for high audience

penetration early in a series, Justin.' For some reason, Clive's comment seemed totally out of place, as did his immediate adoption of Dr Welles' Christian name. Penny felt a prickle of embarrassment and glanced sideways at the doctor. He was regarding Clive in a resigned sort of manner, as though he were long used to having his thoughts repeated straight back at him by less intellectually-endowed mortals.

'Quite,' he commented for the second time that afternoon, in a tone which Penny would have said was laced with studied tolerance. But Clive seemed unaware of this. He grinned and glanced at Penny and Samantha in a self-satisfied sort of way. Penny averted her eyes, but not so late as to miss the look which was approaching admiration on the other girl's face.

'In that case, Justin, I think we can draw up the list for the first three programmes now. Let's review the possibilities,' said Angus Murray. The discussion ranged backwards and forwards for some time and Penny sat quietly and listened. The key people in the team appeared to be Angus Murray, the script-writers, the designer and the doctor. Clive did not appear to be contributing much, although he was insisting that Samantha made copious notes about everything.

It soon became apparent that Dr Welles had a quite extraordinary ability to reach straight to the point of any subject, brushing aside any unnecessary sidetracking in a polite but incisive manner. She had the strongest notion that he had completed people's sentences in his own mind well before they themselves had finished uttering them. In fact, although Jeremy Wheeler was technically chairing the meeting at the head of the table, there was no doubt as to who was really directing the

discussion. She was aware that a happy working relationship was building up among everyone and she felt a
tingle of excitment at becoming part of the team.

She realised that one of the script-writers on her right
was running his hand through his hair in exasperation.
He looked up, sensing she had noticed his confusion.

'It's no good, Sister,' he muttered. 'I really can't keep
up with all these medical terms.'

'I'm sure I can help you with them,' she murmured
reassuringly and leaned sideways to look at his notepad.

'This cauli-whatever-you-call-it. What is it?' He grinned at her. 'Or how do you spell it for a start?' he
whispered conspiratorially. She looked down at what he
had written.

'No, it's not "cauli" as in cauliflower,' she smiled. 'It's
cholecystitis—inflamed gall-bladder. It's spent c-h-o
. . .' She realised she must have spoken at a moment
inappropriate to the discussion at the other end of the
table, for there was a sudden silence which she alone was
breaking. She finished spelling the word in an embarrassed rush. Unfortunately, her companion missed the last
bit and asked her to repeat it. She seized a pencil and
quickly wrote it out on her own pad, relieved to hear the
discussion which she had interrupted resume. Receiving
a murmur of thanks for her help, she sat back and
returned her attention to the meeting.

Dr Welles was staring at her intently, an expression of
puzzled curiosity on his face. So diverted was he that he
seemed unaware of the question Angus Murray was
asking him. His eyes seem to look right into her and
Penny glanced down.

'You're happy with that, Justin?' repeated the
producer.

'I'm sorry Angus. What did you say?'

'I said that we're agreed that the first programme will be concerned with cataracts then, Justin?' repeated Angus.

'Yes, yes. It's a common condition, especially amongst the aged. Also its cure is comparatively simple in its most basic form—and very dramatic too.'

'OK, we're agreed,' said Angus. 'I think the best plan is to refine the pre-production on the first programme and then use it as a model for the later ones. Now, the first thing on the action list is to select the hospital which will be the focal point for the treatment and then the consultant who'll be featured. Although the choice of man is more important than the hospital,' he added.

There was a silence.

Penny recalled that Karen's fiancé, David, hoped to specialise in ophthalmic surgery. He spoke of one hospital with great respect.

'Stanton Eye Unit.'

She realised that she and Dr Welles had spoken the words in perfect unison. He was staring at her with an air of puzzlement again.

'Yes, there is a very good man there,' he said slowly. 'His firm has a tremendous reputation. They were among the first to pioneer transplants of acrylic lenses ten years ago to replace the natural ones affected by cataracts. For the life of me, I cannot recall his name.' He was still staring at her fixedly.

'It's MacMillan,' she said. 'Er . . . James MacMillan.'

'Ah yes, of course. That's it.' He turned to Jeremy Wheeler. 'Your secretaries are to be congratulated. They've certainly done their homework.'

Penny realised she was being grouped with the empty-headed Samantha as some sort of television Girl Friday. She felt a flicker of indignation.

'Oh yes,' replied Angus Murray. 'Or rather, Penny here is actually—' He was interrupted by the door opening to admit one of the LTV catering staff wanting to know if she could clear away the cups.

'Yes, of course,' said Wheeler, glancing at his watch. 'In fact, it's getting on. I think perhaps we've gone nearly as far as we can at this meeting. Let's just tie up the odds and ends and then we can repair to my office for a little further refreshment. I think we've achieved enough today to warrant a toast to the success of the series. Would you be able to join us, Justin?'

Dr Welles inclined his head graciously. 'That would be very pleasant, Jeremy.' He hesitated. 'Actually, I would be most interested in having a look round the studios if that's at all possible.'

'Of course. I'll be delighted to arrange a little guided tour. In fact, in about an hour would be a good time. We put out a local news programme live at six-fifteen, called *London Look-In*. We could actually see that going out.'

'That would be very interesting,' replied the doctor.

Half an hour later found Penny being shown into Jeremy Wheeler's office. Clive led the way over to a cocktail cabinet. 'Shall I do the honours, Jeremy?' he enquired and Penny turned to see the head of documentaries bringing up the rear with Dr Welles.

Jeremy Wheeler's office was imposing, to say the least. It seemed to occupy as much floor space as was taken up by the whole of her sick-bay. At one end was a glass-topped desk with a television monitor to one side. It was turned on and a children's programme was being transmitted. At the other end of the office was a suite of easy chairs and a large settee. The walls were covered with photographs from many TV series which Penny recognised and, glad to have something to focus her attention on, she moved over to investigate them.

'I've worked on quite a few of these as well.' Tim O'Driscoll, the designer, had come to stand at her shoulder.

'Oh really?' she said. 'Which ones?'

He began picking out various shots, but they were interrupted by Clive, wanting to know what they wanted to drink. She asked for a vodka and tonic.

'I remember these wildlife programmes,' she resumed, pointing at a montage of colour prints. Behind her she could hear Dr Welles' voice asking for a whisky and soda.

'Yes, we won a Montreux award for that series,' said Tim. 'Let's hope we do as well with *Life Lines*.' Penny nodded enthusiastically and moved along the wall, with Tim drawing her attention to this, commenting upon that. She liked Tim. He was relaxed and easy to talk to.

Jeremy Wheeler was asking for people's attention.

'Well, if everyone has a glass,' he said, 'I propose we drink a toast to *Life Lines*. Good luck everybody—and to you, Justin. Glad to have you with us.'

Standing in a circle, they lifted their glasses to *Life Lines*. There was an awkward little silence and Penny turned to Tim again, but he was obviously about to be drawn into a discussion with one of the script-writers. She returned to her scrutiny of the photographs, feeling oddly vulnerable. She was aware that Dr Welles' voice was missing from the buzz of resumed conversation and knew he had come over to stand behind her, before he even spoke.

'I expect you're an old hand at all this television mumbo-jumbo?' The tone was light, with a hint of banter and she turned round to face him.

'Actually, Dr Welles, I'm not.' She was fully intending to amplify this reply, but for some reason or another found herself completely tongue-tied.

'Well, in that case, you're remarkably receptive,' he observed. 'You can't have had much time to do any research and I was most impressed with your knowledge at the meeting.'

'Well, I should be able to spell medical conditions at least. I *am* a fully qualified nursing sister.' She had not intended the reply to be so blunt, but something about his condescending manner caused her to feel defensive again.

He had blinked rather at her answer and was surveying her with a fresh interest. 'Are you indeed?' he said, nodding slowly and raising his tumbler to his lips. She caught a glimpse of a snowy white shirt-cuff fastened with a simple gold link beneath the immaculate cut of his suit jacket.

'Is Penelope telling you how I persuaded her to leave dull old St Vincent's and come and work in television?' Clive had joined them. She felt a mild irritation, which grew as he slipped a proprietorial arm around her waist. 'And you're really in the thick of things now, aren't you?' he went on.

Dr Welles had observed Clive's arm, but his face was expressionless. 'Quite a change of career,' he observed. 'And is this your first programme?'

'Oh I'm not permanently on the programme side,' explained Penny hurriedly. 'I've just been sort of seconded. My real job is running the sick-bay here,' she added.

'But that's almost as boring as St Vincent's,' interrupted Clive. 'Apart from a secretary or two with stomach cramps at the wrong time of the month and people like me with the odd hangover, not much goes on down there. Mind you, you did have a sprained wrist to deal with the other day though, didn't you?'

She wrenched herself free from Clive's encircling arm. 'I'll have you know it was a fracture, Clive, not a sprain,' she retorted. 'Actually, it was a Colles'—' She turned to the doctor to correct Clive's fatuous statement, but he was observing them with amusement, for all the world as though he were witnessing a lovers' tiff.

'Anyway, Sister Shepherd saved the situation, eh?' went on Clive and then, rather to Penny's relief, announced that Samantha had just come into the room and was obviously looking for a drink. He excused himself and went back over to the cocktail cabinet.

'Was the hand badly displaced?' asked the doctor, and she looked back at him, still defensive, but found only interest in his expression now.

'No, it wasn't actually. It was more a crack than a fracture. I was soon able to sort it out with the help of St Vincent's A and E department. It only needed a local analgesic and we used a brachial plexus block,' she replied. And then, 'It caused quite a flurry here in the accounts department for a time,' she added.

'I bet.' For a moment, humour danced in the blue eyes.

Encouraged, she went on, 'Is it intended to deal with

all the causes and varieties of cataracts in the first programme, do you think?'

'Well, I don't know.' He paused, eyeing her provocatively. 'I would say that you can contribute as much to that decision as anybody. What do you think?'

She thought for a minute, still slightly suspicious that he was patronising her, then decided to take up the suggestion of a challenge which he had thrown down.

'Well, bearing in mind what you were saying about achieving as wide an appeal as possible with the first programme, I think we should concentrate on senile cataracts for the main theme,' she replied. 'I mean, follow that one through to the simple surgery involved. But if we were also to feature an acrylic lens replacement, say on a younger person, we might be able to show a diabetic cataract case or a heat-caused example—like a steel worker, say.'

'That might be a little contentious,' he observed. 'Such a case could have legal complications if there were any industrial injury claims involved.'

'Yes, that's true,' she replied. 'But surely our aim with *Life Lines* is to show how we can heal? I'm sure we could find a case without any legal problems attached—perhaps one where a claim's already been settled. Anyway, it would make a good contribution towards improving industrial safety.'

'Yes, I see your point,' he acknowledged. 'Perhaps we could find something like that to finish the programme with. The acrylic lens replacement would provide some drama on which to end. Could you mention it to Angus and the writers and discuss it with them over the next week?'

'Well yes, of course.' She was pleased to have his

confidence. 'But don't you want to be involved?'

'I'd like to be, but I have to fly to Switzerland first thing in the morning. I'm away until next Monday and Angus wants a shooting-script put together by then.'

'Oh, I see.' She paused. 'Is it a holiday?'

'Good heavens, no!' he said, a little stiffly. 'I've to visit a clinic, participate in a rather complicated—'

But Jeremy Wheeler was calling for their attention. 'I think we might embark on our little guided tour, Justin, if you're still interested?' Penny blinked. For a few moments she had been so involved in their conversation, she had almost forgotten her surroundings.

'Still very much interested, Jeremy,' answered the doctor over his shoulder and turned back to Penny. 'Are you coming too, Sister? Or is it all old hat?'

'Oh, er, no. I've never seen inside a television studio. Clive's always been going to show me, but . . .'

'Come along, if we hurry we can just get to the control room to see the opening titles for *London Look-In*.' Wheeler was taking Dr Welles' arm. 'You're coming too, Sister? Excellent. Tim, perhaps you could explain things to Sister Shepherd and I'll look after Justin. I'm sure the rest of you have seen more than enough of television studios.'

There was a murmur of assent and she heard Clive saying something about needing to clear up his desk. Tim O'Driscoll stood aside to let her go on ahead, following Wheeler and the doctor.

'Are you sure *you* haven't seen enough of television studios, Tim?' she asked.

'I was going down anyway,' he replied easily. 'One of my sets is being dressed in Studio One and I wanted to check on how it was looking.'

They all took the lift to the big studio complex in the basement of Strand Tower. The lift stopped several times on its descent to pick up homegoers and it was soon quite full. She found herself pressed against the doctor, very aware of his strong frame next to hers. She caught the hint of an expensive cologne. They reached the basement and stepped out of the lift.

'Shall I lead the way? We'll take a look in Studio One first—that's probably the one we'll be using for *Life Lines*,' said Wheeler.

They moved off down a long corridor, their footsteps strangely muffled, and eventually came to a very substantial-looking door. Wheeler swung open a large handle and they went in. It was like stepping into a separate environment, with a strong sensation—almost claustrophobic—of being cocooned away from the outside world. The studio was deserted, although several lights had been left burning. She could not make out anything, except that they appeared to be confronted by a wall of hardboard, rather like some unfinished poster hoarding. They began picking their way along behind it. Wires snaked everywhere across the floor.

'I can't get over how quiet it is,' she whispered to Tim. 'I mean, you wouldn't know you were in the centre of London at all.'

'Has to be this way,' he explained. 'It's the sound-proofing. The sound of a siren from outside or a jumbo jet passing overhead would spoil the illusions a bit, especially if it was during a historical play, like this one. Have a peep round the end of the scenery.'

She did so—and the sense of being in another world was complete. Round the end of the wooden structure she found herself in a Victorian drawing-room, complete to the last detail, from the heavy drape curtains at the window to the aspidistra on the piano in the corner. She stood in the centre of the room and stared about her. She could hear the doctor and Jeremy Wheeler moving about in another part of the set.

'It's part of the ground floor of a Victorian house,' explained Tim. 'There's a hallway through that door.'

She went over to where he had indicated and found a tiled entrance hall, again perfect in every detail, except that the stairs ran up to a landing and then stopped, leading only to the empty darkness of the studio space above their heads.

'Where are the upstairs rooms?' she asked in puzzlement.

'I think that's where Jeremy and Dr Welles are. They're in another part of the set. You can get to them through that front door.' He grinned. 'Strange way of going to bed, isn't it?'

She laughed, opened the front door and stepped out into one complete half of a London street. Jeremy Wheeler and the doctor were standing at the bottom of the steps, looking strangely out of place in their twentieth century suits. She started down towards them, still laughing at Tim's joke, completely failing to notice the lighting cable treacherously coiling itself across the top step.

'I say, be caref—' said the doctor, but it was too late. The heel of her court shoe caught in the wires and she tripped over, pitching forward headlong.

With a jolt which expelled the air from her lungs, she collided with Dr Welles, who had stepped forward to break her fall. Her arms grabbed at his shoulders and a pair of strong hands gripped her waist, gently setting her upright. She found herself looking up into those piercing blue eyes again. Somehow they had lost their luminosity and now seemed almost brooding. Her palms rested against his broad chest and she moved her arms against him, feeling foolish at her clumsiness. For a second she had the absurd notion that he was not going to release her.

'I say, are you all right, Sister?' Jeremy Wheeler's tone was anxious. She was grateful for a reason to break away from Dr Welles.

'Yes. Thank you. How silly of me!' Tim handed her the shoe which had slipped off. Lifting a leg to slip it back on, she again felt the strength of the doctor's grasp as he gripped her elbow to steady her.

Shoes on, she successfully regained her composure, even managing to glance at the owner of the supporting arm to thank him for his gallantry. He inclined his head in acknowledgement.

'I can see we will have to watch our step, Sister, in these unusual working conditions,' he murmured.

She nodded and dropped her gaze, aware that she was blushing. They made their way out of the studio.

Jeremy Wheeler's intention of showing them the control room was thwarted by another party of visitors. 'Didn't realise there were going to be so many people in there already,' he apologised. 'All we can do is take a look through the glass partitioning.'

They did so and she glimpsed a confusing array of controls, tended by several people wearing earphones. On one wall, above the control desks, were banks of television screens, each showing a different picture. She recognised the opening titles of *London Look-In* rolling up on one of the monitors.

'Everything is master-minded from up here,' whispered Tim in her ear. 'Each of these pictures is coming from a different television camera down in Studio Two. The director—that's the one in the middle—can control exactly what picture is being transmitted into peoples' homes by just flicking a few switches.'

Penny nodded, although she did not entirely understand.

'There'll be plenty of opportunity to see over everything properly some other time, I'm sure,' added Tim.

Back in the corridor, Dr Welles turned to Jeremy Wheeler to thank him for the tour.

'It's a pleasure, Justin. I hope it's removed some of the mystery at least—and for you, too, Sister,' replied Jeremy.

'Yes, it has, Mr Wheeler, but I'm still not sure I'll be able to make an enormous contribution. It's all very confusing.'

'But Justin has been telling me about your ideas for the first programme. They sound excellent.'

'They do?' For a moment she felt confused. She could feel the doctor's eye on her.

'Most certainly,' replied Wheeler. 'I'll get the writers to fix up a meeting with you to discuss things. We need to have that shooting script ready to show Justin when he comes back from Switzerland.'

'Oh yes, of course,' she replied, still uncertain.

'I think Sister Shepherd's going to be a great asset, don't you?'

'Yes indeed.' The reply was light and she felt herself being appraised again. 'Well, Jeremy, I have a dinner engagement,' he went on. 'Perhaps I could collect my case from your office?'

She was mildly surprised to find Clive still in Jeremy Wheeler's office, together with Samantha. Either they had been remarkably slow in finishing their first drink or they had availed themselves of another. There was a definite pink tinge to the girl's cheeks.

'Still drinking to the success of the series, Clive?' The head of documentaries' tone was frosty, to say the least. Penny felt an acute sense of embarrassment.

'Just off, Jeremy,' replied Clive. 'Come on Pen, I'll drop you home. The Golf's down in the car park.' He came over to her side and took her elbow. Penny had a fierce desire to shake her arm free but managed to control herself and adroitly moved away, positioning herself on the other side of the coffee-table from Clive. Somehow it seemed very important to conceal the fact that she and Clive had anything but a working relationship.

'Thank you, Clive,' she said over her shoulder. 'But only if it's on your own way home.' There was a puzzled silence from him.

'I should like to thank you for the opportunity to work on *Life Lines*,' she said to Jeremy Wheeler. 'I'm still not sure exactly what will be expected of me, but I shall certainly do my best.'

'I'm glad to have you along, Sister,' he replied. 'And so is Dr Welles. I'm sure you'll be seeing a lot of each other.'

She turned to the doctor to make her farewells, still trying to maintain her composure.

Any intention to coolly wish him a pleasant trip to Switzerland died in her throat as she realised that he could clearly see through her carefully constructed poise. He seemed to be visibly enjoying her discomfiture at Clive's behaviour. She mumbled a hasty goodbye and withdrew with as much composure as she could muster. Clive followed, throwing a casual, 'See you, Sam,' over his shoulder.

Inwardly fuming, but still outwardly calm, she led the way to the lift. Clive seemed to sense that something was wrong, for as they started their descent, he enquired, 'I expect you're glad I fixed you up on the series?' Receiving no reply, he went on. 'Shall I meet you in reception after you've locked up? I thought we could stop off and buy a bottle of wine to have at your place with some supper. Thought I might stay.' He had stepped close to her and was pulling her to him.

'No, Clive, I don't think that's a good idea at all.' She stepped back from him, conscious only of a peculiar air of indifference. She heard the lift bell ping as they reached her floor. 'And in future I would be grateful if you would avoid giving the impression that we have any sort of relationship outside work. Goodnight.'

His face wore an expression of puzzlement as she got out of the lift. Certainly she was gaining a new impression of Clive, she mused, as she tidied the sick-bay office, locked the door and made her way to the back lift in order to avoid any more scenes. She had always assumed that he was competent in his job, but after this afternoon she was by no means sure. She knew that something was going badly wrong with their relationship, something that she could not ignore.

For the moment though, her thoughts kept returning to the unexpectedness of the challenge which had been thrown her and the determination she felt to respond.

CHAPTER FOUR

ALTHOUGH it had been a very full day indeed, she found it surprisingly difficult to drop off to sleep that night. Nor did reading a novel, her normal method of inducing drowsiness, have the desired effect. She found she was reading paragraphs, pages even, without really taking them in at all and kept having to backtrack.

Eventually, realising she must have re-read the opening to a fresh chapter several times, she dropped the book in exasperation and lay back, trying to slow down the procession of disjointed thoughts and recollections which were rushing through her mind. Was it really only twenty-four hours since she had firmly resolved to leave her job at LTV? And yet, in that short space of time, her decision had been completely reversed. She had a strangely disquieting feeling that things were not entirely under her own control.

Even Clive was behaving oddly, she reflected, flirting like that with the Samantha girl. But perhaps she was merely seeing him in a fresh light. She felt a pang of annoyance again at the possessive manner in which he had offered her a lift home. She pursed her lips as she realised how silly she must have appeared to Jeremy Wheeler and Dr Welles—like some callow teenager trying to handle an immature boyfriend. She felt a flush in her cheeks, despite being in the private world of her own bedroom. But what of the challenge Dr Welles had thrown her? She felt a determination to take it up,

especially after the patronising way he had treated her at
their first meeting last week. Despite the interest he had
shown today in her ideas for the first programme, she
still had a nagging conviction that he was merely
humouring her. Well, Jeremy Wheeler had been more
than encouraging and the rest of the production team
seemed to think she could make a real contribution.
She would show the jet-setting Dr Welles a thing or
two, even though she felt very strange in these unexpected new circumstances of television programme
making.

She pondered idly on what reason Dr Welles might
have had for his trip to Switzerland. It must be exciting
to be able to fly off into the blue like that, leaving whole
regiments of people rushing around preparing material
for you to approve when you returned!

She must have dropped off eventually, but woke up
again in the middle of the night and found the light still
on. She switched it off and slept fitfully until her clock-
radio roused her in the morning.

Turning into the entrance lobby of Strand Tower that
day, however, she felt a new sense of anticipation. It was
a beautiful May morning, bright with the optimism of
spring—and the effects of her broken night's sleep had
soon vanished on the walk from the Tube station. She
gave George the commissionaire a cheery greeting as
she stepped across to the lifts.

Up in her sick-bay she tried to put all thoughts of *Life
Lines* and the excitements of the previous day out of her
mind. A lot of things had probably been said in the
enthusiasm of the moment, she told herself as she
slipped on her uniform, checked herself in the mirror
and went to consult her diary for the day's commitments.

Despite her self-imposed calm, however, she practically pounced on the internal telephone when it shrilled urgently a few minutes later.

'Good morning, Sister Shepherd—er, Penny—Angus Murray here. How are you today? All set to help us get the show on the road?'

'Well, I, er . . .'

'Great! Well, Jeremy Wheeler's told me to include you in his script-planning meeting. Says we can't move on anything without you. How's your diary this morning?'

'Well, actually, it's empty,' hesitated Penny, 'but I—'

'Let's say ten-thirty then. I'll round up one of the writers and we'll come up.'

'Up here? To the surgery, do you mean?'

'Might as well. If we're all going to learn about medicine, we ought to start off in the right place.' He paused. 'I take it you've enough chairs for a couple of visitors. It's not all wheelchairs and sick-beds up there?'

She detected a chuckle in Angus's voice and responded in the same vein. 'I daresay I can find a corner for you,' she laughed.

'Fine. See you in an hour then.' There was a click as he broke the connection.

Penny replaced her receiver more slowly. These television types seemed to move at the speed of light. She just hoped they would be patient with her more pedestrian approach to things. She cast an eye round her tiny office. Yes, there was just enough room to hold a meeting with two other people.

At ten-thirty on the dot, the outer door flew open and Angus and the writer whom she had helped with his medical spelling at the pre-production conference appeared. Angus had a clipboard and papers tucked under his arm.

'Fancy some coffee from the machine in the corridor, Sister? Nothing like caffeine for getting the grey matter stirring. Or perhaps you medical experts don't approve of such a feeble need for artificial stimulants?'

'Don't worry, my morning intake of coffee runs to at least a gallon,' smiled Penny. 'In fact, I can offer you the real thing. I've got a percolator going next door.'

Angus and the writer exchanged looks of exaggerated amazement.

'She'll be offering us cocktails made from surgical spirit next,' quipped the writer. 'LTV certainly make sure the medical department's well equipped!'

'Actually, I make it in my own percolator. It was a leaving present from St Vincent's,' she explained.

She returned a few minutes later with a tray of coffee to find the two of them poring over sheaves of notes. She passed them their cups and sat at her desk. A sudden thought struck her.

'Isn't Clive going to be involved in this discussion?' she asked.

There was the briefest of hesitations and then Angus looked directly at her and replied, 'No, I don't believe he is.' His tone was such as to close the subject to any further discussion.

Penny felt a slight sense of relief, but wondered vaguely why he should be excluded. Surely script-planning must be a fairly important subject? Angus interrupted her train of thought.

'Well now, we're all agreed that the first, pilot pro-gramme is to feature cataracts and their treatment,' he began. 'Nobody's had any second thoughts, I hope?' He looked up at the other two.

Penny shook her head. It was extraordinary how they all just seemed to assume she was now part of the production team. Angus was checking back over notes he had made at yesterday's meeting, flicking pages back and forth animatedly, a tiny frown creasing his face. He really was a restless individual and had a habit of hurrying his speech. She had noticed yesterday that all the time he appeared to be listening to other people, he was in reality always thinking about something else. He exuded impatience.

How had the two American cardiologists—Friedman and Rosenman—described the Angus Murray type of personality? Type A, that was it; any person who is aggressively involved in a chronic struggle to achieve more and more in less and less time. Her training led her to decide to try and encourage Angus to slow down a little. Type A behaviour was the surest way to get coronary heart disease at an early age. She had been asked to help produce some medical programmes, not stand by and watch someone on the production team become a patient themselves!

'It's a problem, isn't it?'

She realised Angus was asking her a question about something they had been discussing, the point of which she had completely missed.

'I'm sorry?' she replied quickly.

'I was wondering who should make the first approach to James MacMillan. We should do it today, shouldn't we? How about it, Sister?'

Penny stared at him in amazement. 'You mean you want me to ask him? Invite him to appear on *Life Lines*?'

she gasped. 'But he's one of the country's leading ophthalmologists and I'm just a nursing sister!'

'No you're not, you're acting medical adviser on a major television series. You're highly qualified to make the first contact. We'll follow it up with a formal letter of invitation from Jeremy Wheeler of course, but we always sound people out first.'

'But I know nothing about television! I keep telling everybody that.'

'You don't need to. We'll handle that side of it,' persisted Angus. 'In fact we can sit in on the telephone call.'

'You mean, ring him now?'

'There's no time like the present. Pass me over the telephone and I'll get the switchboard to get the number. Stanton Eye Unit, wasn't it?'

'But he might not be there. He's almost sure to have his own consulting rooms as well.'

'Well, let's start with Stanton, anyway.' Angus was clicking the receiver rest up and down. Penny was about to protest again when she noticed the enormous grin on the script-writer's face.

'There's no stopping Angus once he's got the bit between his teeth,' he observed.

'Yes,' said Penny and reluctantly took the proffered receiver from Angus.

'It's ringing,' he said. The hospital answered promptly and when she enquired if Mr MacMillan was consulting that morning, she was put through to his receptionist with equal speed. She asked to speak to him.

'I'm afraid he's interviewing a patient at the moment. Could you tell me what it's about?' The voice was efficient and rather brusque. Penny hesitated, but receiving encouraging glances from across the desk, plunged on.

'Well, it's Sister Shepherd here, of Leisure Television. I, er, that is, we . . . would like to discuss with Mr MacMillan the possibility of his appearing on a programme we are hoping to make on eye disorders. Cataracts actually. Mr MacMillan is generally acknowledged to lead the field in their treatment in this country and we would very much welcome his participation,' she finished breathlessly, a little surprised at her own new-found tone of authority.

'I see.' The receptionist's voice had warmed slightly. 'Well, you'd obviously need to discuss something like that with Mr MacMillan himself and, as I said, he's rather tied up . . . just a minute though, his patient's just come out. Let me see if I can squeeze you a quick word with him. Hold on.' There was a click.

Penny stared across at Angus, who was watching her face expectantly. 'They're checking if I can speak to him,' she explained and then, in a flash of inspiration, gestured for him to pass across the blue folder from the pre-production conference. She remembered that it contained a very concise description of what *Life Lines* would be about. If the worst happened and he asked some complicated question, she would at least have that to read from. She hoped that she would not become tongue-tied.

The expectancy which filled her tiny office seemed almost too much for its confining walls to contain. All three of its occupants jumped when the receiver clicked again and the receptionist announced that James MacMillan could spare Penny a moment.

The mature voice had an unmistakable Scottish

cadence and was gently chiding. 'Sister Shepherd of LTV, eh? That almost sounds like the title of a TV series in itself. What can I do for you?'

Penny launched headlong into a description of *Life Lines*, referring to the blue folder. She came to the end of her summary and paused.

'Well, that sounds a very interesting project indeed, Sister. But I don't think we can do the subject full justice in a telephone conversation, do you?' responded the consultant.

'No, I suppose not,' said Penny uncertainly, looking frantically at her companions for support. Angus was scrawling a message on his notepad. He held it up. *Is he interested in the basic idea?* it read.

Penny nodded and went on. 'Of course, there would need to be a great deal of discussion, sir, but does the outline sound of interest to you?' There was an almost interminable pause.

'Oh yes, Sister, indeed it does,' he replied. Penny nodded jubilantly at Angus. 'I have a great respect for LTV,' went on MacMillan. 'You ran that excellent series, *Frontiers in Medicine*, didn't you? There's so much ignorance and prejudice about, even in these days of enlightenment. Television can do a great deal to resolve things. But I have a lot of questions I'd need answered.'

Angus was holding up another sheet of paper. *Fix a meeting—A.S.A.P.*

'We could come and discuss it with you, Mr MacMillan. Perhaps tomorrow?' There was another pause and Penny could hear the rustle of pages being turned.

'Could you come down here to Stanton, Sister? My

afternoon list starts at three, tomorrow. I could give you quarter of an hour straight after lunch, half-past two, say?'

'Two-thirty? That would be fine.'

'Until tomorrow then, Sister. Come straight up to the third floor in Windsor block. I'll tell my receptionist to expect you. Good-morning.'

Penny replaced the receiver and stared vacantly at Angus.

'Well? What did he say?' he demanded.

'I'm to go and see him tomorrow afternoon,' she said dazedly. Angus and his companion leapt to their feet and shook her hand.

'That's great, Penny. I just knew you'd be an asset.'

'Well, you'll need to do most of the talking tomorrow, Angus,' she warned.

'Yes, of course,' he replied. 'Wait a minute though. I'm booked to see the rushes of *The World We Live In* tomorrow afternoon.' He thought for a moment. 'Clive can go with you. He should be around.'

Penny thought she detected a note of irony in this last comment. In fact, she did not really welcome the idea of Clive accompanying her when she felt so unsure of things herself. Angus, however, was pounding on with his usual energy.

'Now, let's get the script-writing under way. It's Justin's opening words which are really important. We can handle the general introduction, but we really need some simple background on cataracts, Sister. Can you help?'

Penny considered the question for a moment. 'I think a good source would be some of my elementary training textbooks. They're technical, obviously, but it would give you a start. And I could help with any queries. I'll bring them in tomorrow morning.'

'Penny, you're rapidly becoming absolutely indispensable,' said Angus, and their meeting was over.

Rattling to work on the Tube the next morning, with a bag containing her student books, she ran over in her mind how long it would take her to reach Stanton in time for her two-thirty meeting with Mr MacMillan. She had managed to rearrange her appointments for that Wednesday afternoon and remembered that the eye hospital was down in Surrey. A train from Waterloo would be the best way and she should allow at least an hour for the journey. Better check the times.

She had barely arrived in her office however, when the telephone rang. It startled her slightly, for she always liked to arrive in the lull before nine o'clock and she wondered who else made such an early start. It was Jeremy Wheeler, asking if she could spare him a moment straightaway.

Making her way upstairs to the office, she wondered what had occasioned such an urgent summons. He had sounded most insistent. She reached his office door and found it open.

'Come in, Sister, come in. Do sit down.' He gestured towards the black leather sofa and came round from behind his desk.

'Coffee?' he enquired. There was a percolator on a side cupboard.

'Yes please, Mr Wheeler,' she said. 'White, please, with sugar.' She sat down while he poured her a cup, replenished his own and came over to where she was sitting.

'Well now, Sister,' he began. 'There's been a slight complication with *Life Lines*.'

Penny sat forward in concern. 'Oh no,' she said. 'We are still going ahead with the series, aren't we?'

He smiled reassuringly. 'Oh yes, my dear. Of course. No, it's not that. There's just been a small problem over staff. It's about Clive Shaw. I'm afraid we've had to let him go. Such a foolish young man.'

'Let him go?' said Penny. 'I'm sorry, I don't understand.'

'He's left LTV, Sister. He'd just gone too far. It's a very tough world, television, and there can't be any passengers.'

'I see.' Penny was stunned. 'But what . . . I mean, why?'

'Oh, I'll spare you the details. Let's just say he took one too many mornings off after a night on the town. Strolled into the studios at three o'clock yesterday afternoon, him and that Samantha child. I suppose he just couldn't resist a pretty face.'

Penny hid her confusion by taking a swallow from her cup of coffee. The chief emotion she felt was one of humiliation.

'And of course, it's going to affect you, Sister,' he went on. She stared at him. It was surely inconceivable that they were going to discuss her private relationship with Clive. She felt her cheeks growing red.

'We're going to need you even more on the production team, now. Clive may have been incompetent, but he did do some work. He and Samantha have left a bit of a gap.'

'Samantha has been fired too, then?' she stammered.

'Oh yes. She was only a temporary anyway. Of course,

it's going to put an enormous extra load on Angus Murray and he's asked if you would act as his PA. How about it?'

'But I'm not trained for office work. I'm no secretary.'

'I know that, Sister. Angus already has a secretary,' he smiled. 'No, it would simply be a question of carrying on doing what you've begun. I hear you've already got the country's leading eye specialist practically eating out of your hand. I'm sure you'll be able to handle the meeting with him this afternoon on your own.'

She did not know whether to breathe a sigh of utter relief that her relationship with Clive had passed unnoticed at LTV, whether to mourn the end of that relationship, or to just try and cope with the overwhelming feeling of trepidation she felt at being thrust so unceremoniously in at the deep end.

By the time she was sitting in the fast electric train which was speeding her down to Stanton, the only sensation that remained was an apprehensiveness at the thought of her coming meeting with MacMillan. For Clive she could find only a mild sense of loss. His remarks in the car on the way back from his parents had made it quite clear that he viewed their relationship as entirely casual—and she was somewhat surprised that, when it came to it, so did she.

She could not even focus any feelings of bitterness on Samantha. She was, after all, just a rather vacuous child and presumably had not even realised that Clive had another relationship—nor cared particularly, even if she had known. Samantha and Clive were obviously made for each other.

Jeremy Wheeler had smoothly neutralised her stream of misgivings about her ability to cope with the new

demands of her job. He had stressed how much Angus
Murray needed some efficient and knowledgable assist-
ance and that he hoped she could take some of the load
off his shoulders. This entreaty had struck home with
Penny, who was only too well-aware of the need to
encourage Angus to slow his pace.

She had been anxious to point out that what was being
asked of her was additional to her responsibilities as
Sister in charge of LTV's sick-bay—and that she was by
no means confident that she could deal adequately with
both roles. Jeremy Wheeler had smiled, reached for his
telephone and crisply briefed personnel to book in a
part-time daily agency nurse, pausing only to check
whether Penny thought it best to cover the mornings or
the afternoons. She had opted to have her afternoons
available for work on *Life Lines*, for even her short
experience in television had convinced her that everything seemed to happen in the second half of the day.

As the passing outlook changed from the drab outskirts of London to the fresh spring greenery of Surrey,
she began to relax, the rhythm of the train wheels
providing a soothing background to her thoughts. It
really was an exciting prospect, she reflected. Wheeler
had made it clear that her main role was to liaise with Dr
Welles, to provide a professional medical link between
the programme makers and the presenter. If that were to
be the case, it was essential to be very sure of her ground
at all times. She frowned out at the passing countryside.
The supercilious Dr Welles would take some standing up
to.

Her thoughts moved on to the coming meeting with
James MacMillan. As it happened, her lack of confidence proved totally pointless, for the discussion with

the distinguished ophthalmologist went as smoothly as clockwork. His previously brusque receptionist turned out to be a pleasant-faced, middle-aged lady who responded to Penny's arrival by immediately showing her in to the specialist's consulting rooms. James MacMillan was a breezy character, with hair greying at the temples and a pair of gold-framed half-spectacles.

'Well now, Sister,' he observed genially. 'It seems that an SRN qualification can lead a girl into the most unexpected career developments these days! Do please tell me all about *Life Lines*.'

Immediately set at ease by his approach, she launched enthusiastically into describing the series. She gave him one of the blue folders from the pre-production meeting. He studied it for a few moments and then looked up again at Penny, peering at her over his spectacles.

'Justin Welles is to present the series, is he? I seem to remember sitting next to him at last year's BMA conference. He's making quite a name for himself these days— I'm not altogether sure about members of the profession turning into celebrities, but young Justin's a personable type. He certainly has the looks and charm, hasn't he?' Penny preserved a non-committal silence, inwardly wanting to disagree on the question of charm, which in her experience had been conspicuous by its absence. 'And the idea is to base the first programme on ophthalmology?' he went on.

'That's it, yes. On cataracts, specifically.'

'I see,' mused MacMillan. 'But cataract treatment is very well established now. In fact, the surgical operation involved is one of the oldest in medicine. If you wanted to feature some really up to the minute developments, why not include a case of diabetes mellitus? We're pioneering here at Stanton with the use of laser treatment to prevent the development of ocular neovascular blood vessels in severe diabetic cases,' he said with a hint of pride.

Penny suddenly felt unsure of herself again, but gathered her thoughts and replied, 'Well, actually, I believe the intention is to start the series with some common conditions and then perhaps move on to more complex conditions in later programmes.' She saw that her response had caused him to frown slightly and she hurriedly added, 'But surely we could include a case of an acrylic lens replacement? That's relatively new, isn't it? Perhaps we could find a young case . . .'

'A young patient might well be the *last* sort of case we'd seek for an intraocular implant, Sister.' His tone had developed a definite frostiness and the frown had deepened considerably. Penny knew that she had inadvertently said something to irritate the great man.

'I'm sorry, sir,' she hastened, trying to make amends. 'I don't quite understand . . .'

James MacMillan's expression softened at her obvious candour and he leaned back in his chair, steepling his fingers. 'Get out your notebook, Sister Shepherd,' he said. 'If you wish to persuade me to venture into a television career as well, we will spend the next twenty minutes adding some specialist background to your basic knowledge of ophthalmology.' And that is exactly what they had done, she smiled ruefully to herself later that afternoon, as she stared in bemusement at her notebook, trying to decipher the scrawl.

She had decided not to go back into LTV after her visit to Stanton, but to spend what little remained of the afternoon working at home, determined to draw order into the concentrated flow of lucid information and suggestions that James MacMillan had provided. She knew that the whole shape of the first *Life Lines* programme was contained in her notebook and she was determined to get things straight in her own mind before talking to Angus Murray, let alone Dr Welles.

Several cups of strong coffee later, she had transferred most of her jottings into what was almost a complete plan for the programme. She sat back in her chair triumphant.

The jangle of the telephone was an unwelcome interruption. She glanced at her watch as she went to answer it, seeing to her surprise that it was almost seven o'clock.

'Penny, it's Clive.'

She compressed her lips in annoyance, too surprised at her own reaction to give an immediate answer. She realised that she had not given a single thought to him since that morning's news of his dismissal.

'Penny, are you there?'

'Yes, Clive,' she replied resignedly. 'And I'm rather busy at the moment.'

'You've heard what's happened? It's very depressing. LTV have been really unreasonable. I don't know what my parents will say.'

'I expect you'll find a way of telling them, Clive,' she said coolly.

'I was wondering if I could come round.' There was a pleading note in his voice.

'I don't think so, Clive.'

'Tomorrow, then?'

'I'm busy tomorrow, as well.'

'Well, what about the weekend?'

'No, Clive. Why don't you try Samantha?'

'Are you saying you don't want to see me any more?'

'Yes Clive, I think I am.'

There was a silence and then his voice came again, sulky and resentful.

'Suit yourself then,' he said—and put the phone down on her.

She stood at the telephone table in the flat's tiny hallway, realising that she was shaking slightly. She knew that the trembling she felt was that of anger, not of pain. Yes, she thought, not seeing Clive again really *would* suit her. How could it be that you came to believe you knew a person very well indeed—and then something could happen to prove that you actually knew them not at all? How wrong she had been to think that she was in love with Clive. She realised that an episode in her life was over.

By the following Monday it was almost as though Clive had never existed. The weekend—the first she had spent unattached for some time—was filled with a feeling of freedom, a little overshadowed by thoughts of the forthcoming meeting when the shooting script was to be discussed. The whole team would be there, including Dr Welles.

She was an early arrival in the conference suite and made herself useful pouring cups of coffee for the others as they drifted in through the door. She had taken particular care with her appearance today and was wearing her best dark velvet suit. A crisp white blouse with neatly scalloped cuffs peeped from the sleeves of her jacket and a simple velvet ribbon at the collar contrasted well with the suit. The pair of shiny black medium heels she had bought at the weekend added just the right final touch. She felt smart and confident.

She sensed rather than saw the tall figure come into the room and, determined to get things off on the right foot, went over to where he was being greeted by Angus Murray.

'Good morning, Dr Welles,' she said. 'Would you like some coffee?'

He turned to her with an ill-tempered expression on his face.

'No, thank you,' he growled. 'I'm practically awash with the stuff from the airport.' He turned back to Angus Murray. 'Infernal airline lost my baggage. I waited an hour for them to find it and then had to leave to be sure of getting here through the rush hour. What's the use of getting up early for the first flight from Geneva if you're going to spend the rest of the morning in the arrivals hall at Heathrow?'

'Never mind, Justin. At least you had the wisdom to keep your brief-case with you in the cabin.' Angus had taken his arm and was motioning him towards the conference table.

Penny felt as though she had been dismissed and stood fuming. All her pleasant feelings of anticipation for this meeting had vanished. She had been looking forward to winning Dr Welles' approval for the way she had helped prepare things. She retreated into a subdued silence and quietly took her place at the opposite end of the table to the doctor.

This meeting was obviously to be far more decisive than the first one. Angus Murray took the chair and called everybody to order. He began distributing copies of the script.

'You'll see the sort of opening remarks we've written for you, Justin,' he said. He waited as Dr Welles flipped open the pages and began reading. 'We can make changes if you're not happy with the style.'

The doctor held up a hand for silence while he finished reading the passage concerned. Everything seemed to be hanging on his approval—rather too much so, thought Penny. Eventually he finished his scrutiny and sat back.

'Seems fine to me,' he said airily. 'I might wish to change the odd word, but basically it's OK.'

'Good,' said Angus. 'Now, the next section is where we take the cameras down a hospital corridor to the patients waiting to see the consultant. They'll probably be chatting to one another, perhaps with members of their family present. You'll be out of shot, Justin, but we'll hear you introducing them as we go in for close-ups of each patient. Shall we run through the people we've tracked down who have agreed that their cases should be featured in the programme?'

'By all means.'

'Well, the first involves an elderly lady who is still very active but recently has found that even large print books are becoming difficult to read. Apparently, she is a straightforward case of er . . .' Angus paused and then laboriously read out, 'intraocular cataract extraction.' He looked up and Penny gave him a nod and an encouraging smile to indicate that he had pronounced it correctly. She was aware that Dr Welles had noticed this silent exchange but she chose to avoid his gaze.

'Next, we have a younger man whose family have a history of cataracts developing at an early age. Unfortunately, he is a commercial illustrator and really loves his work. Lately he has found it more and more difficult to deal with the finer details of his illustrations.'

'Any tendency towards colour-blindness? That would be a real problem in his type of work,' interjected Dr Welles.

'Yes, Justin,' replied Angus, consulting his notes. 'As a matter of fact, there is.'

'It's quite a common side-effect of course,' said the doctor. 'There's a theory that the painter Constable suffered from a cataract—it would account for the preponderance of brown in his later landscapes.' He looked round the table as if seeking some response to this knowledgable pronouncement. He really was insufferably pompous, thought Penny.

'And the treatment which is to be recommended for this younger man? Intraocular implant, I presume?'

Angus consulted his notes again. 'No. Apparently it's to be surgery, with a contact lens to be used as the replacement,' he read.

'Oh, surely not!' Dr Welles was sitting forward. 'A young man like that should be recommended for the most modern treatment.'

Angus searched his notes again and, remembering Penny, looked up.

'Sister Shepherd?' he said, his expression indicating that she should answer. She suddenly felt very conspicuous, as everybody at the table turned to her.

'Actually,' she began bravely, but her voice croaked infuriatingly and she had to clear her throat. 'Actually,' she began again, 'that's what I thought, Dr Welles, but apparently it's not always so. In this case, a contact lens is preferable.'

'Is it indeed?' The question, laced with sarcasm, seemed to lie there between them.

Stung by the arrant condescension in his tone, Penny

tried to respond in equal vein. 'That, at any rate, is James MacMillan's judgment.' It had been an attempt at a spirited retort, but it really came out rather mildly.

'I see,' said the doctor. 'Well then, there is no question about it, is there?' He paused and then fixed her with his piercing gaze. 'But do give us a brief background. I would be most interested. Ophthalmology is not my speciality.'

She determinedly drew a deep breath and went on. 'Apparently,' she said, 'or rather, as Mr MacMillan explained, there are likely to be further refinements in the technique of lens implants and this patient has many years left in which to take advantage of such developments by having surgery on his second eye. Also, there can be problems with the intraocular method—chronic inflammation, glaucoma even.'

There was an impressed silence, which even the doctor had to bow to. He shuffled his papers and murmured, 'I see. Thank you.'

Suddenly, concerned that she might have sounded a little petulant, Penny went on. 'Of course, there will be an intraocular implant case in the programme, but it's an older man. He's retired now, but he used to be a glass-blower and has a dense heat cataract in one eye. He's very active, but he has an industrial injury to his hand as well and couldn't really manipulate a contact lens. There are no injury claims involved, Doctor,' she added. 'You remember you were concerned about that at the last meeting?'

He was almost smiling, she observed in amazement. 'Indeed I do, Sister,' he replied.

Completely thrown by this sudden change of mood, Penny fell silent.

'And I take it that apart from supplying the patients, MacMillan has also agreed to be filmed operating on them and actually appearing in the programme?'

Still with her eyes averted, Penny was relieved to hear Angus take this question. However, her relief was rapidly followed by embarrassment as he clearly made the point that the entire credit for persuading the eminent specialist to participate lay with herself. She preserved a modest silence and buried herself in her notes until the meeting moved on to the safer ground of final set-designs, opening music and timing schedules. It seemed that the first part of the programme—the patients' interviews—was to be recorded by the end of the following week.

Only half-listening to the buzz of technical discussion around her, she made a very definite and important mental note. If she was to work successfully with the mercurial Dr Welles, she would have to learn to control the effect his rapid changes of mood had upon her. Not given to such extravagances herself, she found them extremely disconcerting. The meeting broke up and she found herself engaged in discussing some final details with Angus.

CHAPTER FIVE

IT REALLY was just like being in the waiting-room of a consultant's suite in a hospital, thought Penny as she stood, some ten days later, watching Tim O'Driscoll adding the last touches to the set he had designed. She could feel the heat of the television lights on the back of her neck and hear the buzz of voices as the time to begin recording approached. Angus Murray's voice was coming from somewhere behind the scenes, anxiously asking last-minute questions.

'Are Justin and James MacMillan ready? What about the patients? I take it someone's making sure they're comfortable?'

Penny retraced her steps to the specially prepared room where her three charges had been received. She had been unable to resist the temptation to step out and see what was happening on the bustling set.

She returned to find them quite happy and relaxed. The two older ones had brought family along, a daughter in one case and wife in the other. Penny went over to the third patient—the illustrator who was to be treated with a contact lens replacement.

'You came on your own, I see,' she smiled. 'There's probably time for another cup of tea if you'd like one.'

'No thank you, Sister,' he replied. 'How long will we be, do you think?'

'I think they're practically ready for you all now,' she replied, looking at her watch.

'It'll be just as you and Mr MacMillan explained at
Stanton, Sister, won't it?' asked the old gentleman
sitting in a corner with his wife. 'We're just to treat it as
another visit to see the specialist.'

'That's exactly it,' smoothed Penny. 'There are no
right or wrong things to say, just be yourself.'

'Very good advice, Sister.'

She turned, to find that Dr Welles had come into the
room. She was very much aware of his presence as he
came to stand next to her.

'We want everything to be as natural as possible.
You'll find Mr MacMillan will do most of the talking.'
He was addressing everyone now, easily commanding
their attention. 'All you'll find yourself doing is answer-
ing his questions—and they're the same questions that
he asked you when you first met him. Is everybody quite
happy?' There were smiles and nods of assent. 'Well, I
think we might wander through, don't you, Sister? I'll
lead the way. We're going to sit you all down in a replica
of the waiting-room at Stanton Eye Unit, just as I
explained.'

He turned and left the room—a little hastily, Penny
thought, for the previously relaxed atmosphere suddenly took on an air of urgency. The two men quickly
responded, but the elderly lady started showing signs of
agitation. Penny stepped forward.

'There's no rush, Mrs Kehoe,' she said quickly. 'Here,
let me help you.'

'Oh, thank you, dear.' She peered at Penny as she rose
to her feet and it was very obvious she had difficulty in
seeing. She nudged her daughter. 'The nurse'll know
where it is,' she said.

'There's not time now, Mum. We've got to go out

there,' replied the daughter, a rather sour looking individual.

'I'm not going anywhere until I've been to the toilet,' asserted Mrs Kehoe.

'Oh Mum, don't be awkward. You've only just been.'

Penny noted the common signs of tension and quickly intervened.

'Oh, I think LTV can manage to wait for you to visit the loo, Mrs Kehoe. I'll show you where it is. Why doesn't your daughter follow the men and you and I can just pop along the corridor.'

Having satisfied herself that Mrs Kehoe could manage for herself in the Ladies, she sped back towards the studio to explain the delay. Turning a corner, she collided head-on with a tall figure angrily striding in the opposite direction.

'What on earth's holding you up?' barked Justin Welles. 'You're keeping the whole crew waiting.'

Penny gaped. 'Well, they'll just have to wait a bit longer,' she retorted. 'Nature makes more frequent calls on older people, as you should well know. And she's rather nervous about all this television business as well.'

He showed no sign of being appeased by this but actually seemed to bristle even more. 'Well, hurry along, if you please. Angus Murray is getting extremely agitated.'

At this, Penny really bridled. 'Is he indeed?' she flared. 'In that case, I suggest you dash him off a quick prescription for some tranquillisers—before he becomes a patient on his own programme. An episode about hypertension and coronary illness would be very appropriate. Meanwhile, I'll take care of Mrs Kehoe.'

She wanted to add a few further comments about

everybody suffering from first-night nerves, including the supposedly imperturbable doctor, but the words would not come. Instead, she contrived to make a dignified turn and stalked back to collect Mrs Kehoe. She could feel his eyes boring into her back long after she had turned the corner in the corridor.

Eventually things got under way and she found a position for herself well behind the cameras and lights. She was poised to dart forward if she were needed, but everything seemed to be going rather well, although it was not that easy to tell, for the soundproofing in the studio tended to deaden everything and she could not catch all the dialogue. The microphones on their long booms would miss nothing though, she realised as she watched the technicians handling them like enormous fishing-rods. Even the cameras moved around without a trace of sound, like smooth, silent robots, their long lenses probing towards what was happening on the set.

Still smarting from the cavalier treatment she had received from Dr Welles, she could not but help admiring the easy manner with which he faced this daunting array of technical equipment. In fact, were it not for the almost palpable tension amongst those working outside the pool of light which contained Dr Welles, James MacMillan and the three patients, it would be difficult to believe that she was watching a television programme being made—a programme which would eventually be seen in some eight million homes.

She was pleasantly surprised, therefore, when she was asked if she would like to view the recordings—Angus called them the *rushes*—in Jeremy Wheeler's office the following afternoon. She arrived in the by now familiar room expecting the whole production team to be there, but Wheeler's spacious office was empty apart from Angus Murray who was standing at the desk, talking into the telephone.

'I haven't missed everything, have I?' she asked in consternation, as Angus replaced the receiver. 'I had some details to check with the agency nurse downstairs, she's not the brightest I'm afraid, and—'

'Relax, Sister Shepherd,' replied Angus. 'It was only to be you, me and Justin seeing the rushes, but even Justin's going to be late. That was his office on the phone just then, sending his apologies.' He glanced at his watch. 'In fact, that means it'll just be you and Justin to see them. I have another meeting soon.'

She felt a completely inexplicable flicker of unease. 'But surely you need to see them as well. I mean, you're the producer and—'

'I've already run through the tapes once with the others. Downstairs, in video editing.'

'But couldn't Dr Welles and I have seen them down there as well?'

'Well, I suppose so, but it's much better up here. More comfortable. Down in video, it's all metal stools and earphones. I've arranged for them to pipe the tapes up here so that you can see them on the set in the corner. I'll switch it on for you.'

Penny watched him go across to turn on the monitor. It was on a wheeled trolley and he moved it over so that it could be viewed from the sofa. Why she felt so unwilling to watch the video recording with only Dr Welles for company, she could not begin to imagine.

'There we are,' said Angus. 'When you're ready, just ring down and they'll punch it up on closed-circuit. Here's the internal telephone number.' He wrote on a notepad and dropped it on the coffee-table. 'If Justin wants a re-run of any parts of it, or even the whole tape, just let them know. There's no rush. The engineers are all on late shift down there. Justin was just getting into a cab when his office rang, so he'll only be about fifteen minutes. Now, I must fly. Tell me what you both think of the rushes in the morning.' And in his customary headlong manner, he was gone.

Penny sat down on the sofa and picked up a magazine and began leafing through it. She needn't have rushed after all. She realised she had reached the back cover of the magazine but had not taken in a single detail of its contents. She tossed it back on the coffee-table and tried to still the impatience she felt to see the first real results of yesterday's efforts in Studio One. It was extraordinary how this television business got to you! The sense of anticipation she felt was really quite strong. She started when the door suddenly swung open and Dr Welles swept in.

'Ah, Sister Shepherd,' he observed. He had placed undue emphasis on the title and she realised he had not seen her in her uniform before. For a moment, she was about to explain that she had been busy all afternoon and had not had time to change. That would have been too ridiculous, though, for this was a working occasion, not a social one, even if the prospect of sitting in easy chairs and watching what was just a television programme did seem rather bizarre.

Dr Welles had not noticed her lack of response but had deposited his briefcase on the coffee-table and was looking airily around the room. He was wearing a navy blue blazer with plain gold buttons and a pair of light fawn trousers with creases as straight and precise as knife-edges. He looked as though he were starting the day rather than ending it. She rather suspected that he was very well aware of the tailored quality of his clothes.

'Where is everybody?' he enquired.

'The rest of the team have already seen the rushes,' replied Penny. 'It's just you and me who haven't.'

His eyes caught hers. 'And how do we contrive to see this epic?' he enquired sardonically.

She explained about ringing down to the video department. He went over to the desk, dialled the number and issued some terse instructions. She looked expectantly at the television screen but nothing happened.

'They're just lacing it up,' he said and came over to where she sat. The sofa was soft-upholstered and she felt the seat cushions sag as his body sank back into them. The movement seemed to bring her uncomfortably close to him and she shifted her position to make more room, crossing one leg over the other. The television screen remained blank.

There was an almost unendurable silence and she realised that he appeared to be subjecting her ankle, in its crossed-over position near the coffee-table, to the closest scrutiny. Some involuntary instinct caused her to recross her legs in the opposite direction. He leaned forward and picked up a pad.

'Would you mind taking some notes?' he said breezily and she decided his thoughts must have been somewhere else after all.

'Of course,' she replied, grateful for the businesslike air this request had created. The screen suddenly flickered, jumped and then steadied on a picture of a clock face. A tinny voice crackled from the set.

'VTR *Life Lines*. Countdown twenty seconds.' A

pause, then 'Ten . . . five, four, three, two, one—' The familiar LTV symbol and signature tune came up, the picture dissolved and she suddenly realised they were looking at the scenery downstairs in Studio One. It was uncanny, for she could remember that at the recording she had been standing right behind the camera which had taken this shot. But there was not the slightest hint of the studio which she had seen, with all its cables, lights and technicians. Instead, they were clearly looking down a corridor in Stanton Eye Unit. She saw that the camera was moving in on Dr Welles, who was standing to one side of the corridor. Suddenly, his face was in tight close-up. He was leading into the introduction to the programme and she realised with a thrill that he was speaking words which she herself had helped to write.

'For thousands of people, the prospect of failing sight is highly disturbing. But the commonest cause of blurred vision is also one of the most easily cured. That cause is cataracts. Here on *Life Lines* this evening we are going to show you just how they can be treated. You're going to meet three patients from three different sets of circumstances and watch their progress through diagnosis and surgery towards a better quality of life. Let's go along now and see them as they discuss their individual problems with their consultant ophthalmologist for the first time.' He turned and began to walk down the corridor, the camera following at his shoulder.

Penny blinked and had to remember that she was, in fact, watching a video recording. There had been a strange sense of intimacy as she had looked at his face in close-up on the screen. Up till now, she had not noticed the warmth which could suddenly soften the aloofness in his eyes, nor the rather attractive way his mouth could

widen into a smile. It struck her that looking into his face
on a television screen felt considerably more comfortable than in real life, where she found it unaccountably
difficult to hold his gaze.

He was sitting slightly forward on the sofa and she had
to look past him to see the screen. She felt her eyes
drawn towards a study of his profile. He had a habit of
tugging at his chin with his hand whenever, as now, he
was deep in thought. He suddenly turned his head and
looked at her.

'Do you think it's all right?' he asked. 'Those close-
ups are a bit daunting, aren't they?'

For a moment she thought that some vanity or other
lay behind the question, but then saw that the expression
on his face was of genuine uncertainty and knew that he
was as nervous about his appearance on the nation's
screens as anyone else might be, although there had not
been a trace of it in his manner. The question was
disturbingly personal.

'I think it's very good indeed,' she smiled warmly.
'You look absolutely fine.' For a moment, something
indefinable hung between them—and then the self-
assuredness returned to his face and the programme had
moved on to MacMillan's consulting rooms. He returned to devoting his entire attention to the screen, but
this time kept up a stream of comments and observations
which Penny struggled to write down.

'No, I prefer the take without Mrs Kehoe's daughter—she's an unnecessary distraction. Make a note,
Sister, that we must clearly explain the difference between *intra*capsular extraction and *extra*capsular. I expect MacMillan will use phacoemulsification on the
acrylic lens case. It might be a good idea to get the

graphics department to draw up some diagrams to explain it. We can cut them into my voice commentary when we shoot the operating theatre sequence at Stanton. Also, I think we can make it clear that our commercial illustrator patient feels that a contact lens will suit him because his younger brother has been able to use them. People can be very squeamish about fiddling around with their eyes, can't they?' He smiled at her again and then returned his attention to the screen. 'Ah, here comes the link passage for the operating theatre sequence.'

Together they watched his recorded image explaining that the programme was now going to switch to Stanton Eye Unit, where James MacMillan would be seen carrying out the surgery he had just described to his patients. The screen went blank. It was as though a spell had been broken, for she was suddenly very aware again that the room contained only the two of them.

He was looking at her frankly. 'Well, what do you think, Sister?' he enquired. 'Will it make good television when it's actually broadcast?'

'Oh yes, Dr Welles,' she replied with a great deal of enthusiasm, for she really did believe that it would be successful. There was so much rubbish on television these days, it was good to see something worthwhile. And she was contributing to it, she reminded herself exultantly.

Something of these feelings must have communicated themselves to him, for his eyes softened again. There was a pause and she had an odd premonition.

'Well,' he said suddenly, 'I think we can ring down and thank the engineers for screening it and tell them we don't need any re-runs. We don't, do we?'

She shook her head and he went across to the telephone.

'I think Angus should be very happy with everyone's efforts,' he said as he came back to the sofa and began returning papers to his brief-case. 'I never realised how much effort went into making television programmes. Do you think you'd be able to take him through those notes we've made?' He paused and gave a chuckle as he snapped shut the case. 'That is, I'm sure you'll be able to. What I meant was, would you be able to spare the time?' He turned to her again, an easy smile on his face.

This time, her premonition was a certainty. As if from afar, she watched the easy smile on his face turn to something deeper. He caught an arm round her, his other hand slid down behind her shoulder and he pulled her to him, his mouth seeking hers. The abruptness of his embrace made her gasp. His lips closed down on hers and her heart began to pound. She felt herself being pressed back against the sofa cushions, the dark leather cool on the nape of her neck. Her arms futilely pushed against his chest, for she was trying to resist a far superior force. She moved against him but her arms somehow freed themselves and she found that they were resting on his shoulders. She felt crushed beneath him, the soft curves of her breasts straining through the crisp white material of her uniform.

Gradually she felt a warm heaviness suffusing her limbs and knew that her hand had found the thick hair at the base of his head. Against her every will, her fingers began to twist the dark locks.

As suddenly as it had begun, it ended. She lay back weakly as he pulled away from her, his eyes raking hers. Her mind span in a dizzy vortex of emotions. The intensity of his embrace had twisted her cap askew and she vaguely tried to set it straight. His eyes dropped to observe her crumpled uniform and she swiftly sat up, the colour mounting in her neck.

Abruptly, he stood up and in one fluid movement picked up his case, stepped adroitly round the coffee-table and strode over to open the door. In that brief passage across the room, appearing to Penny as if in slow motion, his mood changed yet again. When he turned to her at the door, his expression was a strange mixture— whether of triumph, complacency or sheer mischief, she could not be sure. With her senses swinging back to a more even keel, she glared at him furiously.

'Goodnight, Sister Shepherd,' he said profoundly and was gone, shutting the door smoothly behind him.

She stared after him in amazement, trying to decide whether the outrage she felt was directed at him—or at herself, for not wanting the embrace to end.

CHAPTER SIX

GRADUALLY her pulse slowed to a more controlled rate. But the room seemed to have taken on an unreal quality and as Penny remained sitting on the leather sofa, it became increasingly difficult to accept that the events of a moment ago had actually taken place.

The plush opulence of the office, with its recessed lighting, modern furniture and deep-pile carpet, had the strange effect of making her feel distanced from reality. Seeking some evidence that she had not been dreaming, she reached down and picked up her note-pad which lay on the floor where she must have dropped it.

Without doubt, her imagination had not been playing her tricks, for there were her hurried scribblings and jottings of his dictated comments. She sat back again and stared at the silent television screen. She had been kissed often enough, but she could not recall ever having felt so out of control. Mixed with this rather disturbing thought—which she hastily thrust back down—was the certain knowledge that he had just been playing with her. With his looks and overwhelming confidence, he would probably have no end of women hurling them-selves at him all the time. The fact that she had not must have caused him some puzzlement. Perhaps his male pride had been injured in some way and he had felt obliged to prove something. Yes, that was it. She com-pressed her lips and determined to seek within herself the highest air of disdain with which to greet him when next they met.

The plush luxury of the room had become claustrophobic and she gathered her notes up and left. This floor of the building was deserted, for it was well past hours and the administrative staff would have long gone, although the programme and studio people downstairs would still be working. She went down to her surgery to change into her homegoing clothes and lock up. The ground floor reception was as busy as ever and she realised crossly that she was subconsciously keeping a wary eye open for the doctor. To her relief, there was no sign of him.

It was a beautiful midsummer evening and on a sudden whim she decided to stroll along the Strand and take the Tube from Westminster. The rush-hour was over and she made her way leisurely along, pausing now and then to window-shop.

She reached Trafalgar Square and stepped across at the traffic lights, feeling peculiarly drawn to the summer throng which was promenading around the famous stone lions and swishing fountains. It had been a sunny June day and the air was balmy. The balustrade surrounding one of the fountain pools felt pleasantly warm through the light fabric of her summer skirt as she leaned against it, pausing for a moment to watch the passing scene. A gentle breeze was blowing, occasionally drifting a light mist across the paving from the dancing water-jets. There was that distinctive summer smell when water evaporates off warm stonework.

She breathed a sigh of contentment as she watched the passers-by. The square was busy with people photographing each other, consulting guide books and feeding the pigeons. There were many lovers strolling hand in hand, the girls bare-legged in bright summer prints, their partners relaxed in open-necked shirts and jeans. Here and there were a more formal couple, obviously filling in time before dinner or a show. There was much holding of hands, laughter and the occasional stolen kiss.

A pretty girl suddenly came up to her, holding out an Instamatic camera. 'Excuse me, would you mind taking a picture of us standing in front of one of the lions?' she asked brightly. Penny smilingly took the camera. 'We're on holiday, you see.'

The girl grabbed her boyfriend's hand and pulled him to a suitable position. He was awkward and inhibited, but she took his arm and drew it round her own waist, nestling her face into his shoulder as she turned towards Penny. He relaxed momentarily and Penny pressed the shutter, confident that she had captured a memorable event. It felt odd, recording an intensely intimate moment for two strangers. She passed back the camera to the accompaniment of profuse thanks.

An odd pall cast itself across her previously gay mood. It was ridiculous, almost a pang of envy. Try as she might, she could not regain the earlier magic of the summer evening. She made her way to the Tube.

Her flatmate was full of questions about *Life Lines* and Penny told her how the programme was going, but Karen had to practically drag the information out of her. She went to bed early, making her excuses, but leaving a puzzled expression on her friend's face.

The weekend arrived and with it an event to which Penny had been particularly looking forward. Her mother had always been a lover of the ballet and this abiding passion had communicated itself to her daughter. Last month, Penny had determinedly gone early to Covent Garden on the day when booking opened for the Royal Ballet in Prokofiev's *Cinderella*. She had triumphantly returned with two tickets for this coming Saturday as a birthday present for her mother. They were fearfully expensive tickets. Not the sort of occasion at all which Penny could normally afford to attend. She had only been to Covent Garden once before—to celebrate her own eighteenth birthday. It would be really nice to return the treat for her mother, who would be fifty on the preceding day.

The first half of the performance more than surpassed Penny's hopes. She and her mother had laughed uproariously at the antics of the ugly sisters and watched spellbound as Merle Park breathtakingly danced through the heroine's hopes and dreams for the coming ball, all to the accompaniment of Prokofiev's deeply haunting music. The curtain fell for the interval and she turned to her mother, delighted to see the enjoyment shining in her eyes.

'How delightful, Penny,' she said. 'I'm really enjoying myself—it's a real treat.'

'I'm so pleased, Mum. And isn't this a beautiful theatre? It's so grand. I can only just remember it from when I was eighteen.'

'Yes dear, and on that occasion we also celebrated by buying you a glass of wine in the crush bar! I think we should keep up that custom, don't you? Come along.'

So saying, Penny's mother purposefully led the way out through the rear of the stalls. The barman at the right-hand end of the long bar was always the speediest, she announced, and headed determinedly into the fray. No wonder it had earned the name crush bar, thought

Penny, as she tucked herself into a corner to wait. She surveyed the scene with interest.

Many people were in evening dress and groups were standing together, examining programmes and chattering animatedly. It really was an occasion—and a great success as a birthday present.

Some of the more experienced theatre-goers had obviously learnt that it was as well to order drinks for the interval in advance. A shelf to one side of the bar was set aside for this purpose and Penny idly watched a bottle, unmistakably one of champagne, being removed from an ice bucket by a dinner-jacketed figure.

There was something familiar about the set of the shoulders and as he turned she realised she was looking straight at the unmistakable features of Dr Justin Welles. He had not seen her amongst the press of people, however, and was intent on making his way over to another corner. Awaiting him there, with a welcoming smile on her face, was a very sophisticated creature indeed. She was wearing a dress which, by the look of its expensive cut, must have been bought at an establishment that Penny would probably never frequent, and she was smoking a cigarette in a long, black holder. Her hair was shaped in a simple, but classic style. Surprisingly though, the chief impression which Penny received was one of a rather mature woman, a good twenty years older than herself.

Unable to tear her eyes away from her covert observation—and at the same time rather irritated with herself at this—she watched as the doctor skilfully twisted the bottle and removed the cork with a correctly indiscernible pop. He poured out two glasses and they raised them to each other.

'Here we are, dear. I hope it's not too dry. I asked for a German wine.' The return of her mother startled Penny out of her trance.

'Do you know, I do believe it's the same barman who was here six years ago when we brought you. I'll never forget that magnificent moustache and side whiskers. Why dear, what on earth's the matter? You look as though you've seen a ghost.'

Penny blinked herself back from her reverie. 'Oh, I was just day-dreaming, thinking about the dancing and the music.' This prompted her mother into a torrent of enthusiasm for everything about the production, from the *corps de ballet* to the costumes, and Penny was spared further comment. Despite herself, her eyes kept being drawn back to the elegant couple in the corner. So this was the type of woman to whom Dr Justin Welles was attracted. And it was obvious that he *was* attracted, for he was laughing gaily at practically everything she was saying. They were completely at ease with each other.

She was rather relieved when the interval came to an end. At least she would be spared having to watch them any further. She would not, of course, admit to herself that the sight of them rankled—or that she could have simply dismissed them from her mind by turning her back.

The music of the second half nearly enabled her to recapture her earlier mood, but not quite. She was very moved by the closing scenes though, and the love and tenderness of the hero and heroine—so much so that she found herself fumbling for a tissue as the final curtain fell.

The evening ended in traditional Covent Garden

style, with a devotee high in one of the boxes throwing cascades of roses down upon the principal dancers, with curtain after curtain being taken.

The days passed in an accelerating blur of activity. Jeremy Wheeler pronounced sufficient confidence in the first rushes of the programme on cataracts to authorise script-planning work to begin on the next three productions. She found herself embroiled with the scriptwriters and Angus Murray again, this time dealing with the subjects of arthroplasty, cholecystectomy and kidney transplants.

Of Dr Welles she heard little—until, that is, the day arrived to shoot the second half of the cataracts programme, where viewers would see James MacMillan actually operating at Stanton Eye Unit. Although she had no real part to play at this stage of the programme making, she travelled down to the hospital to watch the shooting. Apart from anything else, she felt that of the three patients, Mrs Kehoe in particular had formed something of an attachment for her and she wanted to wish her well. She enquired which ward the old lady was in and tracked down the Staff Nurse to ask if she could make a brief visit before Mrs Kehoe's operation.

'You'll find her in one of the semi-private rooms. Number seven,' replied Staff. 'You've been working on the programme, haven't you? Mrs Kehoe's told me all about it. She's quite comfortable, had all her tests this morning. She's talking quite positively about everything, says she's looking forward to being able to read properly again. She's going down to theatre in about quarter of an hour.'

'Thanks, Staff,' said Penny. 'I expect all this television business has disrupted things a bit.'

'Theatre Sister was fussing rather, but she always does.' It was said with a giggle. 'She's certainly never had the problem of getting television cameras sterile before. They've only got to be kitchen clean, though. I think there's been a bit of fun, getting the cameramen to wear gowns and masks and so forth. We've been teasing the theatre staff about becoming television personalities!'

Penny laughed and made her way down the corridor. She stuck her head into Mrs Kehoe's room, but only had time to say a brief hallo before the porters arrived to take her down to theatre.

'Of course I'll come and visit you again, but you won't be in here that long,' said Penny, walking beside her trolley towards the lifts. 'They'll have you out of bed and sitting in a chair by tomorrow, you'll see.'

'But I've got to have my new glasses before I go home,' said Mrs Kehoe. 'I keep telling them, but they say it might be weeks before I get them.'

'That's for your final glasses, Mrs Kehoe. *They* can't be prescribed until your eyes have really settled down. But you'll have some temporary glasses straightaway after the operation,' she promised. 'And they'll give you an improvement in your sight immediately.'

Penny knew that all this would have been carefully explained to the old lady many times, but she felt no impatience. Old people could be rather like children. They often needed things repeated by others before they were fully reassured. They reached the theatre corridor and she gave Mrs Kehoe's hand a squeeze.

'Good luck,' she said. 'I'll come and visit you tomorrow.'

'Oh, aren't you coming with me, Sister?' asked the old lady.

'I'm afraid not, but it's perfectly all right. Mr Mac-Millan's all ready and waiting for you. I'll be watching though,' she smiled. She had asked if she could observe all three operations from the lecture gallery, with its glass viewing windows looking down on to the theatre. One television camera had been installed in there on a special staging so that a wide-angle shot of the theatre could be included.

She found Tim O'Driscoll, the designer, sitting in one of the fold-down seats. He smiled a welcome as she sat down beside him but she noticed he looked a little uneasy, unlike his normal irrepressible self.

'I'm not sure I'm going to be able to stay for this, Penny,' he said. 'I stuck my head into the outside broadcast control van out in the car park, but when I saw the sort of close-ups which Angus is going for on those monitors, I thought I'd come up here for a more long-distance view. I haven't got the strongest of stomachs I'm afraid.'

'Don't worry, Tim,' laughed Penny. 'I bet even our capable theatre sister down there swayed on her feet a bit the very first time she was present at an operation. I know I did.'

Only slightly emboldened, Tim returned his gaze to the scene below. Penny could hear a voice coming over the headphones of the cameraman next to her as Angus relayed instructions from his position outside the hospital in the mobile control room.

Everything was in readiness down in the theatre. She recognised James MacMillan standing poised and waiting for his patient. Mrs Kehoe was wheeled in through the flexible double doors and transferred to the table. Penny heard MacMillan explaining over the lecture theatre loudspeaker what was going to happen. As with most modern eye operations, Mrs Kehoe was only to have a local anaesthetic, although she would have had a general injection earlier to help her relax.

They watched as MacMillan asked if his patient was comfortable and then authorised the anaesthetist to proceed. Several injection points were used and after the first tiny sting, it was apparent that Mrs Kehoe could feel nothing. The anaesthetic would affect every local nerve, explained Penny to Tim, including the ones that feel pain, the ones that transmit vision and also the ones that moved Mrs Kehoe's eye. Sterile drapes were placed over her face.

'Of course, the eye actually having the surgery does not see what is happening to itself—because of the anaesthetic,' she said, thinking that this would reassure Tim. Instead, he seemed to go even paler, noticeable even in the semi-darkness of the lecture theatre, and stood up a little unsteadily.

'Yes, well I er . . . thank you, Penny. I must get back to LTV now. Some urgent designs wanted.'

She watched him clamber back up the steep aisle between the rows of empty seats and suppressed a smile. Poor Tim, he would have to stick to his drawing-board and the world of make-believe. She returned her attention to the scene below.

Evidently this was to be an extracapsular extraction and she watched as MacMillan attached the cryoprobe under the cornea and froze it to the lens. He was explaining his every move for the benefit of the cameras. It was not unlike the lectures she had attended as a student nurse. He moved swiftly and surely and had soon completed, performing the peripheral irridectomy to create a permanent outlet for any unwanted aqueous fluid. Penny noticed that he was working with traditional magnification devices for this operation.

For the final operation, however, he announced that he would be using the most modern microscopy equipment. This last operation was to show the intraocular acrylic lens implant and it appeared that viewers would be able to watch his every move, exactly as he made it. She leaned forward, puzzled as to how this piece of surgical and television history would be made. She was so engrossed that she was completely unaware of the tall figure which slipped quietly into the seat behind her.

'He'll use a video-couple,' he said softly and she jumped. 'I'm sorry, I didn't mean to startle you,' he added hastily, gently putting a restraining hand on her shoulder. His action was so spontaneous and concerned that she relaxed in an instant.

'Oh—it's all right. I was just so engrossed in everything,' she replied rather uncertainly, for the memory of their last encounter was still very clear. 'What did you say would be happening?' The practical subject of shared professional interest seemed safe enough ground.

'MacMillan will be using a video-couple microscope,' he repeated. 'It's a sort of miniature television camera but linked into a microscope. It means both the surgeon and the camera can see what's going on at the same time. It's going to revolutionise teaching—just think what a difference a few television screens up here would make. Students would be able to see the whole operating scene and make notes as usual, but they'd have the television for close-ups. And of course, the whole thing can be recorded on videotape and played back later, just as we're going to do when *Life Lines* is broadcast.'

His enthusiasm was infectious and she twisted in her seat, trying to find a composed position from which to talk to him, for the row behind, where he was sitting, was steeply uphill from her position and she had to crane her neck. He was wearing a suit of some expensive tweed material, his lean hands resting on his knees a few inches from her face.

Either observing her awkward position or encouraged by her response—she could not be sure which—he suddenly rose to his feet, towered over her for a moment and then lifted one long leg over the seat-back and, with a loose-limbed scramble, took the place next to her.

'Some contemporaries of mine at Cambridge have developed the microscope,' he said proudly. 'That's it there.' He pointed to a technician manoeuvring a piece of equipment across from a corner of the operating-theatre. 'Of course, the concept's not new, but this degree of miniaturisation had not been achieved before. Cambridge has one of the best microphotography research units in the world. We'll be able to watch our own brains thinking soon,' he laughed.

Penny smiled too, thankful that he could not read her thoughts, for despite herself she knew she was pleased to see him. In one of his open, friendly moods like this, he could be positively charming. The coolness which she had been intending for their next meeting was completely forgotten.

'But why is the video couple so important for this operation?' she asked.

He seemed genuinely pleased to be able to provide an

explanation. 'Well, as you know, MacMillan's going to use phacoemulsification on this patient. It's a way of removing the diseased lens with sound waves. It means that he only needs to make a small incision and it leaves the capsule behind the lens intact. That's important with the newest type of acrylic implants because it provides a bed for them to rest on.' He leaned forward. 'See, there's a television screen also in the theatre so that everybody down there can see what the surgeon's doing as well.'

She nodded in understanding and they watched and listened, heads close together, peering down at the events below. Eventually, with the extraction complete, MacMillan positioned the acrylic lens with sure precision and, fascinated, they saw him suture it with needles barely thicker than human hair. The anaesthetist administered a final anti-inflammatory drug and the operation was over.

Dr Welles sat back in his seat and smiled widely. 'An excellent afternoon for James MacMillan and some excellent television for LTV, I would say,' he pronounced. 'In fact, Mr MacMillan's explanation of what he was doing was so comprehensive and clear, I don't believe my voice-over commentary will be necessary at all. We'll just check with Angus, but I think I may be allowed to go.' He consulted an elegant Rolex wristwatch. 'Plenty of time to get back to London.' He looked at her suddenly. 'Can I offer you a lift?'

'That would be very kind.' The words were out before she had even considered his offer properly. Some warning voice within nagged at her, but as he stood aside to allow her up the aisle she dismissed it. Why not accept a lift? It meant she would miss the rush-hour at Waterloo.

'Let's just go and check that all's well with Angus in the mobile control room,' he said, leading the way out to the hospital car park. The brightness of the summer afternoon outside was a marked contrast to the dimness of the lecture theatre and they walked round to where the big LTV generator was parked with the mobile control room. Cables snaked towards it from an open window in the hospital building, like tentacles from some caged monster. As they clambered up the steps to the unit, the rear door flew open and Angus appeared.

'How about that?' he cried. 'We've made some great television this afternoon. I was just coming to find you two. Do you want to see it on play-back?' His enthusiasm was infectious.

Dr Welles shook his hand. 'Congratulations, Angus,' he said, grinning broadly. 'I must say, Sister Shepherd and I thought things were going very well from a medical point of view. Do you want me for the voice-over?'

Angus looked apologetic. 'Well actually, Justin, old MacMillan was so good, I think we'll leave the sound-track wild. It would be more natural that way. Would you mind?'

'Not at all,' replied Dr Welles. 'In fact, we rather expected you to reach that conclusion, didn't we, Sister?' He was smiling at her.

'It means you've had a wasted afternoon, Justin,' said Angus.

'Oh, I wouldn't say that, Angus,' he replied, but with his eyes still firmly on Penny.

'Come and see the tapes, anyway,' said Angus.

'Well, we were thinking we would make an early start back to London. Beat the rush-hour.'

'That's not a bad idea. I expect the crew would

welcome an early finish,' agreed Angus. He turned and called through the door. 'OK, everybody. Wrap it up.'

They made their farewells and Justin led the way to his car.

'I'm in the visitors' car park across the way,' he said and took her arm as they crossed the busy main road. His grip was gentle, but Penny felt as if an electric current passed between them.

He escorted her over to a rich burgundy coloured Jaguar and, unlocking the passenger door, handed her into the seat. She sat back in the luxurious upholstery. The car smelt unmistakably of real leather and everything was immaculate. It felt brand new. He opened the driver's door and slid in behind the wheel.

'The seat belt's on a reel by the side of your head,' he smiled. She was very conscious of his nearness and found her fingers were fumbling with the snap lock.

'Here.' His cool hand closed over hers and gently clicked the fastening home. 'I think the M3's our best bet,' he said. 'We'll be going the opposite way to the commuter herd.'

He flicked the ignition and there was a soft whine and the engine fired. An astonishing array of dials and gauges came to life on the dashboard. He nosed the sleek, low car out of the exit and waited for an opportunity to join the traffic stream. When it came, he swung the wheel decisively and they accelerated away. She felt a pressure in her back as the car responded. He drove without ostentation, confident in the power of the car, but content to drive within the limitations of the traffic conditions. They reached the motorway and with a gently indrawn sigh, moved across to the fast lane. The miles to London began to drop away. Penny relaxed, enjoying the surge of their passage.

He was concentrating on his driving, for despite being early, the motorway was fairly busy. She too felt no need for conversation. It was odd, the silence between them seemed almost companionable. As if on an impulse, he glanced across at the dashboard clock and checked it against his watch.

'We are going to be back in London very early,' he said. 'In fact, my next engagement is not until seven-thirty.'

She smiled politely, but he was staring straight ahead, a peculiarly hesitant expression on his face.

'I know a rather nice pub down by the river at Windsor.' He was still concentrating exclusively on the road. 'Would you care to make a diversion for a quick drink?'

'That would be very pleasant. I should like that very much.' Surely this voice of eager acceptance could not be hers? She realised it was—and immediately mis-givings filled her mind, but it was too late. The Jaguar was slowing and the soft pulse of his indicator light signified that they were swinging off the motorway.

Ten minutes later they were drawing up outside an inn overlooking the lock at Langbourne. He led the way over to a wooden bench and table near the towpath. She asked for a vodka and tonic and he disappeared into the bar to get their drinks.

Even though it was a weekday, the river was busy and she watched the lock filling up with an assortment of craft. There was much activity, but it was all being carried out at a very leisurely pace. A fair number of holidaymakers were in evidence.

'I always find the river so calm and peaceful.' He reappeared, carrying glasses.

'Yes, me too,' she replied warmly. 'I used to love the water when I was a little girl. We had a stream running through the farm where I was brought up and I was always wandering along it.' She paused, slightly uncertain of herself at this spontaneous revelation of personal details, but he was looking at her with genuine interest. Encouraged, she went on, 'I was a bit of a tomboy, actually. Even had a fishing-rod for a while.'

They laughed together and she realised she had never heard him chuckle openly like that before. It was an easy, relaxed sort of sound.

'Huckleberry Finn!' he teased and she gave a start, for that was what her father used to call her. Still did, when she came back from long walks with the dogs during her frequent visits home. For some reason though, she refrained from divulging this piece of information about herself. It seemed far too intimate. She sipped her drink.

They watched the bustle of activity as the lock filled and exchanged the odd comment about *Life Lines* and how the programmes were going.

'I wish Angus Murray would take things easier,' he sighed. 'He drives himself far too hard. I suppose you have to have people with that sort of energy in television, nothing would ever get done otherwise. But I do wish he would slow down now and again. He's doing himself no good at all.' She nodded in agreement.

A brief flurry punctuated the gentle rhythm of the lock as the gates opened again and the putter of engines heralded the departure of another small fleet of boats unhurriedly nosing upstream. A group of ducks objected to this, however, and furiously took to the air, wings flapping and feet splashing. A chorus of quacks and squawks echoed across the quiet reach.

Penny sighed contentedly. 'Angus should come and sample a little of this,' she said. She knew she was enjoying this interlude immensely and, for the first time, did not feel defensive in his company.

'Yes,' he said. There was a long pause, during which it seemed his attention had moved away from their immediate surroundings. He was staring into his glass. Suddenly he turned to her and she almost jumped. 'Have you ever spent any time actually *on* the river?' he enquired.

She shook her head. 'No, I haven't. Well, not counting the raft my brother and I tried to make once. We got into terrible trouble,' she giggled.

Her anecdote seemed to encourage him, for he went on, 'It's just that I have a boat. It's moored a short way along the tow-path from here as a matter of fact. Quite comfortable. I often take her out for a trip at the weekends. I was wondering if you would like to come?'

Every voice of reason within her warned against the foolhardiness of what she was about to say. This did not in any way cause her to hesitate—or at least perhaps only momentarily—for she heard herself replying, 'I should love to.'

'That's splendid.' His smile was one of real pleasure. 'I was planning to go for a little excursion this coming Sunday. Perhaps you would be free then?'

This time there was no hesitation at all.

'That would be lovely,' she replied.

CHAPTER SEVEN

SHE WAS aware of a slight sensation of recklessness as they completed the journey home from Stanton. Where had her determination to keep him at arm's length gone? Here she was, agreeing to go out with him yet knowing that he was not really her type at all, fast-living to say the least, and a man to be treated with some caution. Despite this, there was a sense of suppressed excitement.

He seemed totally oblivious to her mixture of reservations and anticipation, for he chatted easily on about this and that during the rest of the drive. She confined herself to polite nods and smiles. They drew up outside her Fulham flat and he peered up at the old Edwardian town house with interest.

'So this is where Penny lives,' he observed and she stiffened defensively, expecting one of his patronising comments. But his unexpected knowledge and use of her Christian name indicated nothing but an open friendliness which was echoed in his face as he turned to her.

'Yes,' she replied. 'It's nothing special, but it's convenient and reasonably cheap. I share the top floor flat with my friend Karen.'

'Which is your room?'

'It's the one up under the eaves.'

They both leaned forward and peered up through the windscreen.

'It looks very nice.'

'It's only small.'

There was a silence, during which she continued to stare out at the building, acutely aware of him studying her upturned face. She dragged her eyes back and met his gaze.

'Well . . . until Sunday morning, then.'

'Yes, Sunday,' she replied.

'Do you fancy an early start?'

'Yes, that would be fine. Er, how early?'

He laughed. 'Don't worry, I meant civilised early. Pick you up about nine-thirty?'

'Oh yes, of course. That would be perfect!'

She thanked him for the lift and stepped out of the car. He raised a hand in farewell as she went up the steps to her front door and then was gone in a surge of controlled power.

'Who was *that*?' Karen pounced on her as she let herself into the flat. 'There I was, just happening to look out of the window and up rolls Penelope Shepherd in a Jag. And I just caught a glimpse of what looked like a very attractive chauffeur.'

'It was just somebody from the studio,' said Penny airily, throwing the reply over her shoulder as she went into her room. 'I was offered a lift home.'

'Were you indeed?' Karen followed her and stood in the bedroom doorway, grinning hugely. 'Some lift!'

'Oh, Karen, don't be ridiculous.'

Despite these protestations both to Karen and herself, she knew she was looking forward to Sunday very much indeed. The rest of the week seemed to drag by very slowly, despite the fever of activity which surrounded the planning of the next three *Life Lines* programmes.

Her afternoons were filled with meetings to discuss and explain the mysteries of gall-bladders, gallstones and the surgery involved. There was also the research work needed to find and interview the next patients and their specialists. She was not even able to make her promised return visit to see Mrs Kehoe after her operation, but she rang through to Stanton and found that the old lady was doing well and had been allowed home after a couple of days. Penny wrote her a cheery note and sent some welcome-home flowers with a firm promise to go down and see her in a few weeks' time.

She was able to see snatches of the MacMillan operations and was very impressed with the clarity of everything, especially the microscope shots taken through the video couple. When she enquired if Justin had seen them, she was told that he was very busy and had asked for a video to be sent round to his Harley Street rooms. She realised she did not even know what aspect of medicine he specialised in. In fact, she hardly knew anything about him at all, she reflected.

The weekend arrived and she woke up in an even more carefree mood than usual for a Saturday morning. It was a beautiful day, with that promise of real warmth to come. In fact, it was just the sort of day to buy some new clothes. She swung her feet out of bed, slipped on her dressing-gown and went to put on the kettle.

She tapped lightly on Karen's door as she passed. 'Do you want a cup of tea, sleepyhead? I'm going to brave Oxford Street and buy something exciting. Do you fancy coming with me?'

There was a muffled sort of groan and Penny stuck her head round her flatmate's door. 'I beg your pardon?'

'A cup of tea would be lovely, Penny, but count me

out of the shopping. I couldn't face all those Saturday crowds.'

'What are you going to buy?' went on a slightly more awake Karen when Penny returned with the tea.

'Well, I've been asked out on the river tomorrow and—'

'Have you indeed!'

'Well, yes . . . Anyway, I thought I might look for a new summer outfit.'

'Like that dress you were talking about?'

'Oh, no. I thought something fairly plain and sensible,' replied Penny hastily.

'Nonsense! Go and buy something frivolous. Anyway, what's far more important is who's asked you out?' Karen's eyes were twinkling mischievously.

'Oh, it's only some people from work.' She could not imagine why she chose to veil the truth again. Somehow it seemed important not to give the impression that the outing had any deep significance.

'Lucky you. Well, have fun shopping. *I've* got to go to the launderette.'

Despite her assertions that she was just looking for something simple, she found herself drawn to looking along some racks of figure-hugging jeans and, with only the mildest encouragement from a sales assistant, finally tried a pair on, together with another piece of nonsense in the form of a rather skimpy, but delightfully cool and brightly coloured sun top.

She surveyed herself in the mirror, acutely aware of how snugly the jeans fitted. They were extremely well tailored in stone-washed denim and carried a designer's name. She had managed to lose the winter pallor from her arms by sitting out on sunny days in the back garden they shared with the downstairs flat, so that the top really looked quite good. The jeans went very well with the summer sandals she was wearing and they of course would be perfect footwear for a day on board a boat.

Her eyes travelled up over her neat figure and paused to check the snug fit on her waist. She turned and checked to see how they looked from behind, breathing a sigh of relief that she had never had any real weight problems. The thought that she would be clambering about on a boat tomorrow returned with a new implication. She pulled over the changing-room stool and tried out sitting down, crossing and uncrossing her legs in various positions. She was delighted to see that the jeans flexed comfortably over her slim legs. There were no unsightly bulges and she was confident she could carry off any position, even in the unusual environment of a boat. Anyway, the whole business of boat-handling on the river, as viewed from the pub at Langbourne the other evening, seemed very unenergetic. The greatest exertion required of one seemed to be that of stepping ashore with a rope. And jeans would be a distinct advantage in that respect.

'That looks really good, you know.' The assistant came up to her. 'And the jeans fit perfectly. Don't you like them?'

'It's the top,' explained Penny. 'I seem to be all arms and neck.'

'Well, that *is* the idea with sun tops,' smiled the girl. 'Why don't you try it with your hair down? You've really got to look a bit schoolgirlish with this sort of thing.'

Encouraged, Penny took the pins out of her hair and let it fall to its natural shoulder length. The girl was right. She did look about sixteen, but the effect would be very good, especially when her hair was freshly washed and brushed out. She made up her mind and bought the clothes, adding them to her credit card account with mild abandon.

Karen insisted on a full dress rehearsal that afternoon, accompanied by even more insistent interrogations as to whom Penny was going out with. She remained non-committal, thankful that Karen was doing an early at St Vincent's the next morning and would be prevented from teasing her even more when Justin arrived to collect her.

The day promised to be another scorcher and she decided to take only a light cardigan with her. She had woken early and showered and washed her hair, brushing out the ash blonde strands until they shone. She paused to make a final check before running down to answer his knock. She felt free and unencumbered in her new jeans.

He had been very prompt—nine-thirty on the dot. As she opened the door, she was acutely aware that it was very important to her that he would like her outfit.

The effect on him was quite marked. She felt an impish thrill of satisfaction as she saw the expression on his face, for he was practically gaping. For a moment, she thought she'd overdone it, for his eyes dropped to her *décolletage* and then lower as he moved back to survey her full length. She thought he was going to step back over the top step, so genuinely was he taken aback.

'You look tremendous,' he said, grinning mischievously.

'Thank you,' she replied and sought a diversion by pretending to check if she had her key with her. She had,

of course, checked the contents of her handbag count-
less times already that morning.

He had slid back the sunroof of the car and she was
glad, for she was very aware of him as he settled in the
driving seat. The open roof seemed to add exactly the
right feeling of freedom and lack of confinement to the
day. His clothes matched this mood as well. He was
wearing a pair of light linen trousers and smart blue deck
shoes and his shirt sleeves were rolled back casually to
the elbows, exposing lean, brown arms. Soon the Jaguar
was purring down the motorway towards Langbourne,
its slipstream now and again causing a downdraught to
ruffle her hair through the open roof. It was a pleasant
sensation.

'We can leave the car in the inn car park, again,' he
said as they reached their destination. 'I know them
quite well and they don't mind. Besides, the chef's a
friend of mine. Runs an excellent kitchen. Actually, I'm
just going to collect the most important item of boat-
ing equipment from him now.' Slightly puzzled, she
watched him disappear into a side entrance of the
inn.

He emerged a few moments later, triumphantly
carrying a wicker hamper. He beamed at her as he set it
down and locked up the car.

'Lunch,' he announced.

'Lovely.'

'Right then, I'll lead on. The mooring's a hundred
yards or so upstream.' They set off. The morning was
still and quiet and as yet there was no river traffic at all.
The surface of the water was like a mirror.

'It's going to be really hot, today,' he said over his
shoulder.

'Yes,' she said. 'I love the sun. Do you?'

'Very much. It's so good to get outdoors isn't it, after being shut in all week?'

'Yes, it is. It's very nice of you to ask me.' She was looking down at her feet as they picked their way along the rough path and nearly collided with him, for he had stopped and turned.

'It's nice of you to come,' he said simply. 'Well, here we are.' She realised they were standing next to a long hull moored alongside a wooden jetty.

'Oh,' she exclaimed in delight, 'It's a narrow-boat!'

'Yes, and a genuine old wooden one at that. I've done a lot of the work to her myself.' There was more than a hint of pride in his voice and justifiably so, thought Penny, as she gazed at the boat. It was very long indeed. There was a cockpit at one end which contained the steering tiller and woven rope fenders hung along the length. A line of little windows with neat curtains ran down the side next to the bank. The woodwork was painted a shiny green and the panelling was decorated with a profusion of flowers painted in bright, primary colours. The centre panel bore the name of the boat in intricately decorated lettering.

'*Lass of Langbourne*,' she read. 'What a lovely name!'

'I'm glad you like it,' he said with a grin. 'She used to be a butty boat,' he added.

'Sorry?'

'A butty boat is the one that was towed behind the main narrow-boat,' he explained. 'It was used for carrying the cargo.'

'I see.' She examined the boat again with fresh interest. 'So all the bits on top—the cabin and everything—have been added.'

'Yes—to my design actually, although I've tried to keep to the traditional styles.'

'Yes, I can see that.'

'And of course, I've had an engine put in. She used to be horse-drawn.' He ran a hand through his hair, as though his own spate of enthusiasm might have seemed too effusive. 'Anyway, shall we go aboard? I'll go first. The gang-plank's quite steady, but don't trip over the mooring-lines:'

He walked up the plank with a couple of easy strides and turned to take her hand as she followed and jumped down to join him in the cockpit. The boat rocked gently, reminding her that they were now afloat. He gave an easy smile of approval at her sure-footedness and she returned it. She knew with a light skip of her heart that today was going to be very memorable.

'Well now,' he said. 'Let's stow the vital ship's provisions and I'll show you round. Then we might as well cast off on our little voyage. You'll find that I've added quite a few mod cons.'

He pulled a key from his pocket and unlocked the double doors to the cabin. A short companionway led down below. A pleasant smell of warm timbers and varnish rose from within. She passed the hamper down to him and then hesitated for a moment as she realised that negotiating the steps backwards in her close-fitting jeans presented something of a problem. He had, however, chivalrously turned his back and was moving down inside the cabin, pulling back the curtains at the windows.

'I'll just turn on the fridge,' he said.

'Fridge?' she echoed incredulously as she reached the bottom step.

'Yes,' he said, turning back to her with a nonchalant smile. 'It runs off container gas. Quite simple. So does the central heating!' Conscious that simply repeating these revelations back to him might seem faintly ridiculous, she managed to contain her amazement this time.

'There's a special gas system for which I buy refill containers—and the system's just like a domestic one, only much smaller of course. Same sort of principle applies to the hot water and the loo. There's even a shower,' he laughed.

'Goodness,' she cried, 'you could almost live aboard the whole time!'

'As a matter of fact, I try to most of the time, but things always seem to keep me in London. Especially recently, with *Life Lines* and all this television work. Anyway, I'll just attend to a couple of mechanical things down here and then we can get going.'

Ten minutes later, they were gently moving away from the bank, the deck vibrating to the slow thud of the diesel engine under their feet. She had made herself ready to help with the casting off, but he handled everything himself, making it seem like child's play.

'I'll do it myself the first time, so you can see what's involved,' he had explained. 'In any case, it's mooring up and going through the locks where I really need the crew.' He had grinned and swung on the tiller, reaching out a foot with a well-practised movement to kick the engine lever into gear and apply a touch of throttle. There was that air of contentment about him which comes from the familiarity of often-repeated pleasures.

She turned and faced forward, finding a comfortable position standing on the top step of the companionway, her arms resting on the cabin-top. The movement of their passage raised a gentle breeze which touched her bare skin.

As they moved away from the boatyard at Langbourne, the riverside buildings began to thin out, giving way to large and elegant houses with terraced gardens leading down to the water's edge, many with boathouses in which craft of all shapes and sizes nestled, the sunlight playing in dappled reflections on their shiny hulls. Above the rhythmic tonk of their engine, she could hear the occasional quack of ducks and, as they moved into the open countryside, the soft cooing of wood-pigeons. The river began to widen and meander through broad meadows with stately willows lining the banks, their tresses reaching down to trail in the water. And all the time there was the gentle gurgle and trickle of the water as it played along the narrow-boat's hull. Penny could feel the warmth of the gradually strengthening sun seeping into her shoulders. It was all absolutely idyllic.

Gradually the slowly changing vista on either side of them began to weave its spell. She found herself completely relaxed in his company and when he asked if she would like to brew up some coffee, she responded eagerly. Following his shouted instructions, she quickly found the ingredients and flicked a light to the gas under the kettle. The galley was spotlessly clean and neat. Certainly, he did not appear to have the more casual approach to housekeeping of most bachelors. But then of course, this was a boat and perhaps, as such, set higher standards than the normal domestic environment. She hummed a little tune to herself as she waited for the kettle to boil.

'I'm afraid we'll have to postpone the coffee, Penny.' He was shouting down to her and she looked up to see his face in the companionway entrance. 'There's a lock coming up.'

She turned off the gas and clambered back up to the cockpit. He had slowed the engine and was looking ahead, shading his eyes against the midday sun. She followed his gaze. Up ahead of them was a small gaggle of boats waiting to enter Langbourne Lock. From their own level, down here on the water, the big lock gates looked enormous. As she watched, they began to swing open and another flotilla of craft came out, heading downstream.

'We're going up river, so it will be empty as we go in. Then they'll fill it and up we'll go, just like a lift. Have you been in a lock before?'

She shook her head. He had engaged forward gear again and they were gently approaching the entrance.

'Can you manage to look after things at the bow?' he asked. She nodded, although by no means sure what would be expected of her. But she need not have worried for his explanation was crisp and clear.

'There's a boat-hook up there on the deck and as we come into the lock you'll see some loops of chain hanging down from the walls. As we stop, just grab one of the loops with the boat-hook and steady us. You'll find a coil of rope up there as well and the lock-keeper will probably ask you to throw it up. He'll pass it round a bollard and give you the end back. Then all you've got to do is take up the slack as we go up. I'll do the same at this end. Think you can manage?'

She nodded, although by no means sure what a bollard was. She need not have worried, though, for everything went like clockwork. Sure enough, there was the friendly face of the lock-keeper looking down at her from the top of the lock wall and she managed to throw the rope straight and without tangling it. A number of cabin cruisers joined them in the lock and they exchanged greetings. Many admiring glances were cast at *Lass of Langbourne*.

The lock began to fill as the keeper opened the sluice-gates to let the water swirl in from the next level. They began to move upwards, the dripping, weed-covered walls sliding down past them. She fended them off with the boat-hook and cast an eye back to the stern to check whether she was doing the right thing.

He was sitting on the cabin roof, effortlessly using his outstretched legs to stop them bumping against the stonework. He was wearing a broad grin and obviously approving her seamanship. She smiled back happily.

They were elevated almost to the top of the lock now, back out in full sunlight, and the rush of incoming water had slowed to a trickle. Other boat-owners were freeing their bow ropes from the bollards. She waited for Justin's instruction and flicked their rope easily free as he called. She heard the familiar rumble of the engine and they puttered out onto the next reach of the river as the gates opened. She coiled the rope and made her way back along the deck to the stern.

'Well done,' he said. 'You're an excellent crew.' She looked at him suspiciously but there was nothing in the blue eyes except friendliness. 'I hope you're enjoying yourself,' he added.

'Oh yes, I really am!'

Their eyes held each other's for a moment and he cleared his throat suddenly. 'I'll finish getting the coffee. Here, you take over.'

Before she could protest, he had stepped away and

clattered down to the cabin. She made a dive for the tiller in case they should suddenly swing off course, but she need not have worried, for they simply continued on as before.

'Just lean against it to turn in whichever direction you want to go,' he called up. 'Try a few experiments. It's very easy.'

She did as he suggested and grasped the long, smoothly polished arm. Despite its length and unwieldy appearance, it had a sensitive control over the boat and she tried a few pushes and pulls, watching how it affected the direction of the boat's bow. The flotilla which had emerged with them from the lock seemed to have dispersed and they had the water to themselves. In fact, when he returned with the coffee, Penny even managed to steer with one hand and hold the mug with the other.

Gradually the morning passed in a delightfully relaxed manner. As they came round a wide, sweeping bend in the river, he pointed up ahead.

'That's our lunch place,' he announced, indicating a group of willows, themselves part of a copse set at one end of a lush, green meadow.

'It looks charming,' she said, eyes shining.

A short time later found them snugly moored to two ropes slung from the trees, with the gang-plank easily spanning the narrow strip of water which separated them from the bank. A picnic blanket and cloth were soon spread on the grass, with an assortment of crockery and cutlery from the galley, and he sat down to rummage in the wicker hamper.

'Let's see what the Langbourne Arms has packed for us,' he said. Penny knelt down on the blanket to peer inside too.

'I do believe they've done it again,' he laughed, lifting up one container after another. 'Smoked salmon—even with some slices of lemon. Then cold chicken, ham and a really excellent salad. And strawberries and cream to follow.' He looked at her with all the delight of a schoolboy foraging in a tuck-box. 'But I almost forgot the most important thing.' He sprang up and strode back up the gang-plank, returning a moment later with a bottle of white wine and two glasses.

'*Liebfraumilch!*' exclaimed Penny. 'My favourite. And it looks lovely and cold.' She watched as he deftly withdrew the cork and poured it out, the glasses misting almost immediately. He passed her one and raised his.

'To the *Lass of Langbourne* and a beautiful summer's day,' he said and they drank the toast together.

The meal was every bit as good as he had promised. They ate their way slowly through the courses with frequent expressions of delight, the cool wine slipping easily down with the delicious food. She felt no obligation to make artificial conversation, but soon found herself telling him about her parents' farm and how she had first wanted to enter nursing. In return, he told her a little about himself, how his father had wanted him to join the family business but how, in the face of substantial paternal opposition, he had insisted on medical college.

'And now you're a press and television personality,' she chided—a little daringly, for she still felt rather unsure of herself with him.

'Yes,' he replied ruefully. 'That's OK as long as it doesn't interfere with my main interest.'

'I was wondering what aspect of medicine you specialised in,' she prompted him.

'It's plastic surgery, actually,' he replied. 'I'm keen to try and bring standards here in England up to those of the Swiss and French.'

'Your trip to Geneva?' she recalled.

'Yes—and I have a clinic in the burns unit at Orford. That keeps me busy quite a lot of the week.'

She nodded in interest. He was lying on his side, his head propped relaxedly on one bent arm. She was sitting upright, her legs neatly folded beneath her on the blanket. Here, under the trees, they were in the shade and the light breeze, which occasionally set the willow branches moving around them, gently reached in and touched their faces.

'Mmm,' she said. 'That was an absolutely fabulous lunch.'

'It was good, wasn't it?' he agreed. 'Actually, I'm quite drowsy.' He lay back on the blanket. 'I apologise in advance if I should drop off,' he murmured.

'Same here,' she laughed and followed his lead. It seemed a very appealing idea to lie back dreamily and gaze up at the chinks of blue sky discernible through the gently shimmering leaves. Somewhere, high up above them and invisible, a skylark dropped down its liquid, bubbling notes.

She must have fallen asleep for a little while, or at least reached that delightful state of enervation halfway between slumber and wakefulness, when something caused her to open her eyes and her heart leapt as she saw his face, a breath away from her own. He was studying her features intently, a quiet smile playing around his mouth. With the inexorability of something that is meant to happen, he lowered his head and covered her lips with his. It was gentle at first and she felt

herself melting beneath him. Her arm discovered a will
of its own and moved gently on his shoulder. He was
lying at an angle to her, supported on his forearms.

But then suddenly his kiss became far more insistent
and against every voice of reason she found herself
responding. His tongue was probing her mouth and she
could feel the solid bulk of his shoulders beneath the
fingertips of her hand. He moved his head and traced a
burning line of kisses down the arch of her neck and
across her breast. Through half-closed eyes she could
see the branches above her. At the periphery of her
vision were the tall blades of grass around the edge
of the blanket. They seemed odd, viewed from this
angle, almost towering over her. Her heart was beating
wildly.

His head returned and he buried his cheek next to
hers, breathing her name in her ear. She felt his arm slide
round her waist and he pulled her roughly to him, his
mouth seeking hers again. She found her body responding, could feel his hard muscular strength pressed
against her.

Suddenly, a stronger breeze set the willow leaves
dancing afresh and their loud rustling filled the air. It
seemed to break the spell. She pushed against his broad
chest with her free arm. At first her movements were
futile, but then suddenly he broke away.

'Justin, please, I can't . . . I mean—' she stammered.

He was staring at her fixedly, the pupils of his eyes
enormous. Abruptly he ran a hand through his hair and
twisted away, drawing up his knees to his chest, and sat
staring out across the sunlit meadow, his back towards
her. She suddenly felt rejected.

'I, er . . .' He cleared his throat. 'I'll go and put the

kettle on for some coffee.' He stood up and, without a backward glance, went back on board the boat.

She lay there for ages, her heartbeat racing. This situation was exactly what she had wanted to avoid. And yet, she knew that the ache his embrace had aroused within her was not going to go away.

She sat up, a little shocked to see that the sun top was in disarray. She quickly tweaked its wayward strap back on to her shoulder and frantically sought some activity to be engrossed in when he came back. She became aware of a gentle quacking from the water's edge, accompanied by a softer, cheeping sort of sound. She rose to her feet and, a little vaguely, went to investigate. A pair of ducks were slowly paddling their way amongst the reeds and accompanying them were half a dozen tiny floating bundles of feather and down. She pretended a deep engrossment in this charming family scene, whilst listening for the sound of his returning feet on the gang-plank, and willed the wild beat of her heart to slow down.

He seemed to be taking ages to make the coffee and she moved slowly along the bank, following the parent ducks and their brood. Eventually she heard him coming back and felt her heart beginning to pound again.

'Here,' he said gruffly and practically thrust a mug of coffee at her.

'Thank you,' she replied and drew his attention to the ducks, glad of the diversion they provided. His mood had completely changed however, for he obviously did not share her pleasure at the scene.

'Aren't they beautiful?' she persisted. 'I'm going to give them the remains of the bread from our lunch.'

'Please yourself,' he replied. 'I'm going to clear up.'

Without waiting for a reply, he turned and strode back to the willow trees and began repacking the hamper. She had the strongest impression that she was irritating him in some way and felt confused and hurt.

It was as though a veil had been drawn across the day. The colours seemed less vibrant, the warmth gone from the sun. Out of the corner of her eye, she saw him carry the lunch basket back on board. He must have registered her remark about the surplus bread, however, for it remained, pointedly, on the picnic cloth. She went to retrieve it.

She returned to the river's edge and knelt down, tossing morsels to the ducks who greeted them with ecstatic quackings. It was an enchanting scene. Why wouldn't he share it with her? She could hear him clumping up and down the gang-plank again. Men always had to turn a perfectly enjoyable day into a *situation*, she brooded angrily. This morning had been absolutely idyllic and the lunch perfect. Why should a gentle embrace cause such a reversal? And yet, she knew it had not been simply a gentle embrace. She had wanted him to kiss her and had responded with equal fervour—until things had begun to get out of hand.

Well, she was simply not that sort of girl, she reminded herself. If Dr Justin Welles was accustomed to including love-making under the willows as a normal part of his river excursions he had got hold of the wrong girl for today's trip. She rose to her feet and brushed the breadcrumbs from her jeans.

She found him in the galley stacking crockery in the sink.

'I'll do the washing-up,' she offered, a little hesitantly, still unsure of his mood.

'That's kind of you. I'll go and cast us off then. We should be making our way back.' She could not help feeling a pang of disappointment, for his comment added a finite quality to the day. Despite everything, she did not want it to end.

'Do you want any help casting off?'

'No, thank you. I believe I can manage.' He disappeared up the companionway. His tone was now one of rather formal politeness. He had obviously found a mid-point between the charged intimacy and frosty aloofness of a while ago. An absurd notion crossed her mind that she almost preferred the earlier stormy atmosphere, but she shrugged her shoulders and busied herself at the sink.

Soon they were sliding back down the river and eventually a series of bumps caused her to look out of the window and see that they were returning through the lock. She hurriedly finished drying the last cup and ran up the companionway to help.

She need not have rushed, however, for he was standing amidships, nonchalantly handling both bow and stern ropes, one in each hand. He had not noticed her head bob up and she hurriedly ducked down. She felt that he would have again refused her offer of help and somehow she did not want to feel unneeded. It would have been painfully disappointing after their companionship this morning.

She went back through to the salon and flopped disconsolately down on the cushions of a side berth, idly perusing a row of books in a side locker. One caught her eye. *Stanford's River Thames Guide—Langbourne to Oxford*. She flipped through the pages, pausing here and there to look at the pictures. She heard the engine cough into life and the lock walls slid past and gave way to the river view again. She swung her legs off the side berth, determined to enjoy the last of the day as they slipped back down river to Langbourne. The book fell from her lap and fell to the cabin floor, fluttering open at the title page. She bent to pick it up, unable to miss the handwritten message on the flyleaf—

To Justin, In memory of a wonderful weekend. Not that he needs a guide—to the River Thames or anywhere! Fondest love, Helen.

Penny felt a wave of bleakness wash over her. Miserably, she tried to tell herself that of course this was the sort of man Dr Justin Welles was, that of course she had been stupid to believe that they had been sharing something special on this beautiful summer's day. A man like him would have no end of girlfriends, have had no end of love affairs too. He probably looked upon her simply as a light diversion with which to amuse himself on a free Sunday.

She stayed below for the remainder of the trip and said little as they stowed things away and made the boat fast before leaving for the drive back to London. Her mood seemed to match his and they drove like strangers. She thanked him politely for a pleasant day, finally summoning the courage to look him in the eye. To her surprise, however, their eyes barely met before he averted his gaze, mumbling something about having enjoyed it himself. She stood on her top step and rather forlornly watched him drive off down the road.

Some time in the middle of the night she woke from a restless sleep and found her cheeks wet and the pillow damp. In that strange world of suspended consciousness, in the dark of her room, she knew that she was falling in love with him and that there was very little she could do, or wanted to do, to prevent it.

CHAPTER EIGHT

THE CERTAINTY of what had happened to her was still there when she awoke the next morning—a strange elation which was immediately swamped by gloom as she remembered the true nature of the man who had so overwhelmingly swept into her life.

Even Karen, not normally the most observant of people, noticed that Penny seemed a little subdued. She felt her flatmate giving her an odd look as she retired back to her room with her morning cup of coffee and restricted her replies to the barest minimum when asked about her river trip.

Nor did the bleakness lift as the next few weeks passed, despite the fever of activity leading up to the production meeting about the next three programmes in the series. Apparently the board of LTV had given their approval for the first programme about cataracts to be transmitted and now it was all stops out to get the rest of the series under way. She found herself buried in the by now familiar process of briefing script-writers, liaising with consultants and interviewing patients.

Were it not for her preoccupations with Justin, she would have acknowledged that she was enjoying herself more than at any other time in her life. Her earlier fears about dealing with the ultra-sophisticated television types had completely evaporated by now. They were all very charming and extremely witty and intelligent. She came to realise that she gained completely the wrong impression from Clive. How long ago all that seemed.

She was acutely aware that Justin would be at the forthcoming production meeting and was looking forward to seeing him very much indeed. She knew how futile such feelings were of course, but something inside kept prompting her to give in to them. She was determined that her contribution to the programme making would be absolutely impeccable and threw herself into all the intricacies of arthroplasty, kidney transplants and cholecystectomy, which were the topics to be featured.

She had been particularly fortunate with the cholecystitis subject for she had found a highly appropriate case from St Vincent's. The patient concerned had been prone to a serious weight problem and, as is common, the gall-bladder condition had followed. She had been put on a low-fat diet and some of the symptoms had diminished—but cholecystography had shown that the gall-bladder reaction was impaired, indicating the likelihood of stones being present. Surgery had already been recommended and the patient's agreement obtained.

Penny had really enjoyed the visits back to her old hospital, especially in her new role. The registrar who dealt with biliary system surgery at St Vincent's had the reputation of being a bit of a fire-eater with his firm and she had had frequent brushes with him when she had been running men's surgical. It was good to have the tables turned slightly, for it was obvious that he viewed appearing on television with some trepidation. She derived a certain amount of glee from actually adopting the role of reassuring the great man.

There had been very little news of Justin during the weeks leading up to the meeting. She knew he had been in touch with Angus from time to time, for she saw draft scripts going to and fro, often covered with notes and comments in his distinctive handwriting. However, she was not aware that he had actually been into Strand Tower for any discussions.

The day of the production meeting arrived and she sped along the corridors, her notes and files tucked under her arm. She had been looking forward to it all week, conscious that she had done her part very competently. This morning they would be going through the final scripts and shooting schedule. She ran over again in her mind the provisional arrangements and dates she had made with the various hospitals, specialists and patients. She hoped everybody would approve. Especially Justin.

The meeting was being held in Jeremy Wheeler's office and she found nearly everybody already assembled. She shut the door behind her and made her way over to the group seated round the coffee-table. How confident she felt compared to her very first introduction to this office all those weeks ago when they had drunk a toast to *Life Lines*!

There were friendly greetings from the rest of the team and space was made for her on the long leather sofa. Angus and Tim O'Driscoll, the designer, were poring over final set designs which were spread out on the coffee-table and Jeremy Wheeler was deep in a telephone conversation at his enormous desk at the other end of the office.

'Well, that's all agreed, then,' Tim declared as he rolled up his plans. 'I think I might as well duck out of this meeting, Angus, get the set-builders cracking on this lot straightaway. I take it you've got the most important person's approval on these designs?'

'Justin Welles, you mean?' asked Angus.

'No, Sister Shepherd, of course!' Tim gave her a large wink and a grin and disappeared out of the door. Penny leaned her head back and returned his grin with a smiling shake of her head. The mention of Justin and the sensation of the cool leather against the nape of her neck reawakened the memory of another episode in this office, involving just two people, an episode which had ended in a far from businesslike manner. She thrust this image away from her and engaged in small talk with her colleagues, but a large proportion of her attention remained on the closed door, waiting for it to open and admit, for her, the most important member of the team. She was slightly puzzled, therefore, when Jeremy Wheeler finished his telephone conversation and, pulling his large executive chair over to join them, suggested that they make a start.

'But aren't we going to wait for Just—er, Dr Welles?' she asked. It was apparent that she had voiced the question uppermost in several people's minds, but she had not intended it to come out in quite such a precipitate fashion. Jeremy Wheeler blinked at her in a rather surprised manner.

'Well no, Penny. Actually, I was just about to explain. He's in Paris. I'm expecting a call from him before the end of the meeting. He may have some rather exciting news.' He beamed round at everybody. She refrained from further comment, fearful that she might draw more attention to herself. She knew she was very disappointed that he was not coming after all.

Copies of the script for the cholecystitis programme were distributed and she dragged her attention back to matters in hand, although even this did not put Justin from her mind, for the first words she read were, of course, his introductory remarks.

'I say, this has been really cut, hasn't it?' she observed.

'In what way, Penny?' Angus was staring at her.

'Well, I mean, I'd thought it was appropriate to describe how much cholelithiasis has increased in western countries recently. It's all this fat we eat. I mean, it's absolutely galloping away in America.'

Angus cleared his throat uncomfortably. 'Er, I, that is Justin and I, weren't sure it was relevant, Penny,' he said.

'Not relevant?' echoed Penny indignantly. 'People need to be reminded that tipping all this fatty food down their throats certainly isn't the best route to a healthy body.'

'There is a definite link then, Sister?' interjected Jeremy Wheeler. 'I mean, between standards of living and chole—er, gallstones?'

'Absolutely,' said Penny emphatically. 'I mean, during the last war, in Holland, where there were virtually no fats in the diet because of rationing, gallstone symptoms dropped to almost vanishing point. You should see the figures now.'

'I see.' He paused and then turned to Angus. 'I think we might raise the subject with Justin again.'

'By all means,' replied Angus.

They passed on and Penny subsided into silence again, aware that she might have made a bit of a fuss. Still, she knew she was right. People paid far too little attention to what they ate. Dr Justin Welles should know that, but perhaps he had more pressing things on his mind—like gadding about in Paris.

The meeting passed from one subject to another and

Penny knew she was hardly paying sufficient attention. She responded well enough when the schedules were being discussed and everybody seemed to find her suggestions regarding the cases to be featured more than adequate. Despite all this, however, most of her attention was poised to hear the phone ring, following Wheeler's remarks about a possible call from Justin.

When it did come, she jumped perceptibly, as one often does when an intensely-awaited event actually occurs. Fortunately, her companions on either side did not seem to notice anything. Jeremy Wheeler crossed to his desk and perched on the corner.

'This may be the confirmation I've been expecting,' he observed, as he picked up the receiver.

'Ah, Justin!' he exclaimed. '*Comment allez-vous? Ah oui, en Anglais.* That was the limit of my schoolboy French, anyway,' he gave a chuckle. 'What's the news?' There was a pause, during which everyone gazed expectantly at Wheeler. He was nodding, interspersing the stream of conversation he was hearing with comments— 'Splendid.' 'Excellent.' 'Yes, I understand.' He looked back at his audience at the other end of the office and raised his hand in an expression of triumph. Everybody exchanged puzzled looks.

'Yes, Justin, that's perfectly clear.' He paused again, obviously listening to a question. 'Yes, yes. Absolutely fine. We've practically finalised all the arrangements. We're all clear for your project. Oh, there was just one small point.' Wheeler's eye had alighted on Penny and she felt a flicker of embarrassment. 'Sister Shepherd had a query about the openers for the gall-bladder programme. Yes, the dietary aspects . . . Well, she's here now. Why not discuss it with her? Right. Yes. Keep in touch, my boy.'

He stood up from the desk and motioned for Penny to come over and take the receiver. It was the last thing she wanted, to have a disagreement with him in public. There was no escape, however, and she rose reluctantly to her feet and went over to the desk.

'Might as well sort out the problem now,' smiled Wheeler. 'Don't take too long. There's something exciting to tell everybody.' She took the proffered receiver.

'Dr Welles?' she said diffidently, for this was the first time she had spoken to him since their day on the river.

'Good morning, Sister.' His voice came over the line. 'What's the problem?'

'Well, it's not a problem, really.' Good heavens, she sounded positively mouse-like after her earlier outburst. To make things worse, it was obvious that Wheeler was waiting for her to finish before imparting his news to the meeting and everybody was listening. She drew a deep breath. 'It was just the beginning of the cholelithiasis programme. I thought it would be a good opportunity to remind people about the dangers of overeating. I mean, it is appropriate and the Health Education Council's spending all this money telling people about the importance of a sensible diet and—'

'I quite agree, Penny. I can't think why it's been left out. Could you sort it out with the script-writers?'

She was dumb-founded. 'Well, of course—'

'Good. Well, I must dash. There's a lot to be organised. Wish you were here to help. Never mind, I shall see you on the seventh.'

'The seventh?' Her mind was in confusion—partly because of the warmth in his voice, partly his ready acceptance of her suggestions and partly at this future date which he seemed to assume she knew all about.

'Jeremy will explain. *Au revoir!*' There was a click as the connection severed. She replaced the receiver in a daze.

'Everything agreed? Good!' Wheeler was beckoning her back to the meeting. 'Well now, everybody. Let me put you in the picture. As you all know, Justin is an exceptionally talented plastic surgeon. I have been trying to get him to feature in an actual operation himself to provide a climax to the current series, but he has always resisted. He says that he would need a perfect case, one where the background was not merely cosmetic and so forth. He says that so many people still believe that his skill is only of interest to ageing film stars and pop singers.' He paused for effect. 'Well, it seems that there is a tragic case in Paris, on which he has been asked to consult. Some of you may recall that young English girl who won the York Piano Competition . . .'

'Yes, I do,' interjected Penny. 'Wasn't she involved in a terrible car crash in France soon afterwards? Such a beautiful, talented girl.'

'That's quite correct, Sister. She suffered multiple injuries, including severe burns to her forearms and backs of her hands. Also her face. Well, apparently she has recovered from the worst effects of the accident, but the burn scar tissue on the backs of her hands will inhibit her playing—she has lost her suppleness. Also, there is the question of her confidence—will she appear in public again with the damage to her face? It seems that Justin, in consultation with the Marie Frambére clinic in Paris, who have a special burns unit, believe that plastic surgery can be of help. Justin has agreed to operate and to have the operation featured on *Life Lines*, providing it is successful. It means of course that we would do things in reverse, that is, shoot the operation first and then backtrack over the preliminaries. And we have very little time.'

'How little time?' Angus, ever the worrier, was leaning forward anxiously.

'Ten days,' replied Wheeler. 'The production team will fly over on Thursday week. I'm planning to do an Intervision link-up with our friends in Télévision National Francais. We'll just fly out the key people—everybody in this room, that is—and a crew for the actual recording of the operation.'

'But Thursday week is the day after the press preview party to launch the series. We'll have to come back from Paris and immediately start on shooting the gall-bladder programme for next month!' Angus was looking positively distraught.

'That's absolutely right, Angus,' replied Wheeler smoothly. 'But I know you all love a challenge.'

There was rather a stunned silence and then a buzz of conversation, although everybody seemed far more concerned to rush away and get on with their individual responsibilities. The meeting broke up, leaving Penny feeling slightly breathless.

The last thing she had expected that morning was to hear that she was going to Paris in ten days' time. She felt a thrill of excitement. Apart from the occasional package holiday, she had never been able to travel a great deal and Paris was a city she had always wanted to visit. A hundred things seemed to be clamouring for attention in her mind—her passport, for instance, was it out of date? What should she take to wear? She realised she did not even know whether it was to be a one day trip or a stop-over—and then there were all the myriad details to be taken care of from the meeting.

She found herself back in her sick-bay office after leaving the meeting, without even recalling how she had got there. She leaned across her desk, flipped open her diary and pencilled in these new events. It rather looked as though she would have to get the agency to supply a full-time nurse during next week. Nor had she realised she was invited to the press preview party until this morning. It was to be held in the hospitality suite upstairs. She returned to the question of wardrobe. Perhaps she would wear the silk jumpsuit she had last worn at St Vincent's May ball, it was just the right mixture of formal and dressy. After all, the invitation had said that drinks and canapés were to be served, so the preview was certainly to be something of an occasion.

Her thoughts moved on to the Paris trip. She would need to have something smart to wear on the plane—and then, if there was to be an overnight stay, there might well be an evening function as well.

As the day of the press preview drew nearer, the feeling of excitement amongst the *Life Lines* production team seemed to intensify. Although everybody was very confident about the first programme featuring cataracts, the seal of approval from the TV critics was still vital. Certainly the rate of acceptances to the launch party invitations had been high and it was obvious that the series would attract a lot of interest.

Penny had arrived in the hospitality suite early, despite knowing that she would not really be able to answer any of the technical television questions. To her surprise, however, she found herself being taken into tow by Jeremy Wheeler and immediately engaged in conversation by one of the leading Sunday newspaper critics. Jeremy was exactly the right person to take her under his wing, for he simply exuded confidence and she found herself responding to the medical questions fluently, despite the rather daunting sight of people making notes of what she was saying.

During a lull in the proceedings, she turned to Angus Murray and voiced the question which had been uppermost in her mind all day.

'Is Dr Welles coming?' she enquired.

'Oh, rather. He's coming in on an evening flight from Paris.' Angus craned his neck over the assembled throng. 'As a matter of fact, that looks like him now.'

She felt a sudden lift in her heart. A small voice of reason nagged within her at this foolhardy sense of pleasure at the prospect of seeing him again, but she smothered it and tried to peer through the crowd. She caught a glimpse of his head, topped with fine, dark curls, and the flash of his white teeth as he exchanged greetings with people.

Angus was beckoning to him, but Jeremy Wheeler's next words shattered Penny's pleasure with an unintentional but harsh brutality.

'Oh splendid. He's brought Helen with him.'

It was as though she had suddenly been drawn out of her surroundings. The buzz of conversation around her seem to recede and take on a brittle, hostile note. It was ridiculous, she almost felt betrayed. She could see Justin clearly now. He was skilfully making his way through the crowd, leading an extremely attractive woman. In a flash of recognition, Penny realised she was looking at his companion from the ballet at Covent Garden and in the same flash of recollection was the memory of an inscription in sophisticated female handwriting in a guidebook on a narrow-boat's bookshelf. So this was Helen . . .

Her eager anticipation of seeing him had changed in an instant to fierce disappointment. She felt an urge to run away, but somehow remained rooted to the spot. The elegant pair joined their circle.

'Hallo, how was the flight?' asked Jeremy Wheeler.

'Routine,' replied Justin easily. 'But fortunately I had Helen for company.'

'Oh, you were both in Paris, then?'

'Not to start with, darling, but we decided to combine business with a little pleasure.' Helen's voice was mature, a little husky—studiedly so, thought Penny—and she regarded the company from under suspiciously long eyelashes, then began delving into her handbag for a cigarette to fit into the long black holder she was brandishing.

'Have you met everyone, Helen?' asked Justin solicitously. This attentive side to his nature was quite surprising, thought Penny angrily. So this was the real reason for his lengthy stay in Paris. She glared at Helen.

'Jeremy you know, of course—and Angus Murray. I don't think you've met Penny. Helen Lampard, Sister Penny Shepherd.' He made the introduction with practised ease. They exchanged greetings.

'Sister, did you say?'

'Yes, Penny's a nursing sister. We've roped her in to help with the series and now she's practically indispensable,' smiled Justin.

Penny found that this patronising manner of his was even more insufferable than the airs and graces of his rather superior companion, who had meanwhile received this information with an exaggeratedly polite nod and then turned her attention to Angus, asking him for a light to her cigarette.

On a sudden impulse, Penny excused herself on the pretence that it was time to circulate again with trays of canapés, despite the room being full of waitresses. She withdrew abruptly from the circle, not noticing the rather puzzled expression on Justin's face.

Over by the bar, she found Tim O'Driscoll in a group with the script-writers.

'Hallo Penny,' he said. 'Have you come to talk to the really interesting people?' He bent his head in a conspiratorial whisper. 'I don't know about you, but I can't bear all these media types. They seem to talk at each other rather than with each other.'

'I know what you mean,' she replied. Tim's breezy greeting had blown away her gloom. She found herself drawn into a cheery group of writers and designers, even allowing another glass of wine to be pressed on her. In a surprisingly short space of time, she noticed that there was a general movement beginning through to the viewing theatre where the video of *Life Lines* was to be shown. She attached herself to the rear of the party, still in Tim's company.

It was a small theatre, equipped with easily enough comfortable seats for the thirty or so people present. The front ones were already filled as they came in and she and Tim made their way up the aisle. They would pass Justin, who was sitting at the end of a row with the Helen woman and Jeremy Wheeler.

'Are you going to come and sit with me at the back then, Penny?' Tim was speaking to her in a mock-intimate way, taking her arm. She could feel Justin's eye upon her and some irrational impulse made her return Tim's mild flirting.

'Only if you promise to behave,' she giggled and patted his hand. She walked past Justin's seat, pointedly ignoring him, although she knew he was registering her every move.

By the time they found some seats though, she was having regrets. The last thing she wanted to do was encourage Tim. Good heavens, she hadn't behaved like this since she was a schoolgirl. She resolved to keep herself under control for the rest of the evening.

Jeremy Wheeler made some opening remarks and the lights dimmed as everybody turned their attention to the several monitors that were placed in the room. This was the first time that Penny would see the complete programme and she settled back to watch with a growing sense of pride as the opening titles came up. Some special introductory music had been recorded for the series and she was fascinated to see the ingenuity with which the graphics department had designed the opening message. It was in the form of an electrocardiograph trace on the screen of an oscilloscope. With each pulse, the moving green blip made up a letter—until the title *Life Lines* filled the picture. Then the words dissolved and she found herself once again looking at the striking features of Justin Welles as he introduced the cataracts programme with the skills of someone who might have spent their entire career in the television profession. Again, she found the detailed close-ups of his face very disconcerting.

The audience watched in rapt attention and when the action moved to the microscopy shots at Stanton Eye

Unit, she could hear impressed murmurs from those around her. The programme drew to an end and as the LTV symbol reappeared on the screens, there was a spontaneous ripple of applause. She turned to Tim, who was wearing a broad grin.

'I've never been to one of these previews,' she said. 'Would you say that was a good reception?'

'Very much so,' he replied. 'They're a hard-bitten lot, these critics. I think we'll get some good reviews. Mind you, we won't know until we see the programme notes in the Sunday papers.'

'After we get back from Paris,' she added.

'Yes, that's right.' Everybody was getting to their feet and she and Tim also stood up. 'Are you looking forward to the trip?' he went on.

'Yes, very much,' she replied levelly, knowing that she should not appear too effusive in case Tim should think she was encouraging him further. His next words, however, set her mind completely at rest.

'My girlfriend's absolutely green with envy. She's always wanted to go to Paris and is demanding I bring her back a really expensive present to make up for leaving her behind. I don't know what to get her. Do you think you could give me some advice?'

'Well, I'll try, Tim,' she answered with a smile, but her tone was vague, for she had just noticed that the seats which had been occupied by Justin and his companion were now empty. They must have slipped out just before the end of the programme. She realised Tim was talking to her again.

'How are you getting out to the airport in the morning, Penny?'

'Well, I hadn't thought, really. What time's our flight

again?'

'Eight-fifteen, Air France. Angus and I have organised an LTV car. There's a spare seat, if you like we could pick you up. You live out our way. West London isn't it? Give me your address and we'll collect you at seven.'

The reminder about tomorrow's early start prompted her to take her leave. She still had a few last minute items to pack and she wanted a good night's sleep in order to be refreshed enough to enjoy the trip. She collected her coat and started homewards.

As she turned the corner from Strand Tower, one of the LTV limousines which she had seen waiting outside the building swept by. In the gathering summer twilight, she could make out the profile of Helen Lampard in the back seat, engaged in laughing conversation with Justin Welles. Penny turned towards the Tube, quickening her step as she did so.

Karen, her flatmate, was full of questions. 'How did it go, Penny? It all sounds fabulous. I've been reading that copy of the script which you left me. And now you're off to Paris, you lucky thing.'

'Yes, it is all rather exciting.' Penny smiled at her friend's genuinely shared pleasure.

'I say, I didn't realise the programme was being presented by Justin Welles,' added Karen with a knowing shake of her head. 'He writes a column in *Eve* magazine, doesn't he? I don't have to warn you about him, I'm sure.'

Penny stiffened slightly. 'What on earth do you mean, Karen?'

'Well, he's got quite a reputation at Orford General, you know.'

'Orford? Isn't that where he has a burns clinic?' enquired Penny, trying to sound casual.

'Yes, that's right. One of the Orford theatre sisters has just moved to St Vincent's. I was telling her about *Life Lines* at coffee and she was telling me about Dr Welles.'

'Oh, really?' Penny's tone was unbearably casual, but her every sense was willing Karen to continue.

'Yes. There've been a few casualties amongst the hearts of the nursing staff at Orford I can tell you. It seems he plays the field rather. There's some rumour about him having a tragic past, never wanting to settle down with anyone again and so forth.' Karen began collecting up their coffee-mugs to take out to the kitchen. 'Still, no need to tell you to beware. You're far too level-headed. Anyway, I expect you've had enough of men for a while—after Clive I mean.'

'Absolutely,' uttered Penny with forced emphasis, but the hollowness in her heart seemed to echo right through her reply.

CHAPTER NINE

SHE HAD set her radio alarm for six o'clock but was awake a long time before. The dawn light filtering through her brightly coloured print curtains had awakened her, she decided, although if she were truthful she knew it was the excitement of the Paris trip which had pulled her from her fitful sleep.

She dressed quickly and was ready in plenty of time for when the car was due. She saw it turn into the top of her street from her sitting-room window and, picking up her suitcase, she flew down the stairs before the driver had even reached the front door. Somehow, being up this early added an extra dimension to the departure. The summer sun was already warm on the shoulders of her smart navy blue linen suit as she gave the driver her case and went down to the car.

Tim was standing by the rear door, holding it open for her. She slipped into the back seat and he joined her. She exchanged greetings with him and Angus, who was sitting in front and heard the thump of the boot lid as the driver stowed her baggage. Her companions seemed to be feeling the same sense of excitement. Angus was wearing his permanently anxious expression but was trying to concentrate on the morning papers. He offered her one, but she did not want to assume the air of the blasé traveller and sat back in her seat, not wishing to miss a single moment of this experience. There was an intoxicating feeling of going away, strangely reminiscent of years ago when taxis came early in the morning to whisk her away as a child on exciting family holidays. They sped through West London, the streets still quiet before the hubbub of the day, and up on to the motorway link to Heathrow Airport.

Next to her, Tim suddenly gave an exclamation. 'Well, we've made the gossip columns at least,' he laughed. 'I bet Justin will be furious.'

Somehow, Penny knew she did not really want to know what Tim was referring to, but she could not help turning to him with an expression of curiosity. In any case, Angus was leaning over from the front seat, trying to see what had caught Tim's attention in the paper.

'It's the Simon James page,' he explained. 'Listen.' He started reading aloud. '"Distinguished plastic surgeon Justin Welles's name is linked more and more these days with that of Helen Lampard, journalist, critic and much-invited London dinner party guest. Last night, the couple were to be seen at The Berkeley, obviously celebrating something. Could it be Dr Welles's forthcoming debut as presenter of *Life Lines*, LTV's new medical documentary series? Current personalities in television should look to their laurels, for *Life Lines*—and Dr Welles—promise to provide us with compelling viewing."'

Penny's two companions greeted this report with a certain amount of merriment, but she could only join in half-heartedly.

'Well, it's our first publicity for the series and it sounds good, even though it is mostly about Justin,' remarked Tim.

Angus seemed pleased. 'I knew he was a good choice as presenter. He'll get us the ratings, I know.'

They reached the airport and swiftly went through the routine of checking in. Penny had never travelled on a scheduled flight before—her earlier journeys had been on charters—and soon found herself enjoying the atmosphere of Air France. There was not the feeling of being processed which normally pervaded a package holiday journey. Croissants and coffee were served for breakfast and she began to enjoy the feeling of being abroad.

There was no sign of Justin amongst the passengers and when she asked about him, Angus explained that he was catching a later flight. Probably sleeping off the aftermath of his celebration last night, brooded Penny disconsolately, but gave a shrug and determined again that any brush with Dr Justin Welles was not going to detract from the pleasure of the trip. She knew that the ache she felt each time his name was mentioned would not go away for a long time. It was all absolutely hopeless, she told herself, she would never have any place in the sophisticated life that he lived.

She was diverted from these rather gloomy thoughts by some concern about Angus Murray. She was the first to admit that she herself was not the best of air travellers but Angus, sitting next to her, seemed to be working himself up into a real state. During take-off she had noticed his hands, white-knuckled, gripping the seat arms like grim death and he had not even touched his coffee. By the time they began their descent to Charles de Gaulle airport, he was positively ashen, beads of moisture standing out from his brow. She tried to divert him with questions about their destination, but could not make any impression.

'Sorry, Penny,' he muttered. 'I just hate flying. Just

hate it.' By the time they had landed, he was physically shaking. She was very concerned, for this degree of stress was not good for anyone. It was almost worth enquiring about alternative methods of travel home. The train and hovercraft could not take much longer, she reflected. But then Angus was probably the type to work himself into a state about anything.

By the time they had disembarked, he had regained a little of his colour and the architecture of Charles de Gaulle airport served to provide a welcome diversion. The building was futuristic, to say the least. At one stage they had to travel on escalators encased in clear plastic tunnels. Other escalators and walkways crossed and recrossed the building at the most extraordinary angles and they burst out laughing at the sight of two other members of the production team travelling in a similar transparent tube, but in the opposite direction. They were obviously lost and their silent-film gestures and mimed questions across the intervening space were very amusing.

They were met at the exit terminal by a minibus from TVNF and were whisked away to a briefing meeting at the French television company's headquarters. Despite having learnt a healthy respect for city traffic from her years in London, Penny was rather unprepared for the headlong manner in which French drivers propelled their vehicles around. The coach swayed and swerved and the horn appeared to be an essential aid to progress, none of which helped Angus's state of mind at all. Penny was rather disappointed that their route seemed to be taking them through the outskirts of the city, for she had hoped to see some of the sights for which Paris was famous.

Eventually, they arrived at the offices and were warmly welcomed. The morning was spent discussing the plans for recording the operation. This seemed to take a great deal of time for there were several language difficulties. Fortunately, Angus spoke fairly good French and was kept busy translating the technical points. She was glad to see that this served to completely take his mind off their journey and he was soon almost back to his tensely energetic self. The operation was to be performed the next morning and it looked as though they would have the evening to themselves for sight-seeing. This afternoon they would visit the Marie Frambére clinic so that Angus and the production people would be able to inspect the outside broadcast arrangements.

'It'll be organised on much the same lines as the Stanton recording,' Angus explained. 'Penny, I'd like you to station yourself in the viewing gallery again, but this time please could you make detailed notes of everything. As Justin himself is doing the operation with a French team, he may get too involved to explain to the cameras in English what he's doing at every stage and we may have to add some commentary afterwards—' He was interrupted by a stream of comments from the French technician and he paused to listen, nodding from time to time. He turned to Penny again.

'It is being suggested that you should actually be in the control room with me so that we can advise on camera angles and so forth right on the spot. What do you think? It's a good idea, you know. After all, we've got to get it right first time. You can't exactly rehearse this sort of thing.'

'Yes, I could do that,' she replied a little hesitantly.

'But I'm rather uncertain as to exactly what techniques Dr Welles will be using. It's a pity he couldn't be at this meeting,' she added ironically. 'I'm not really an expert on plastic surgery.'

'Perhaps you could go through it with him this afternoon,' suggested Tim O'Driscoll. 'I understand he's going to meet us at the clinic after lunch.'

'Oh, I see. Well, in that case, yes of course,' she replied, furious with herself at the feelings the thought of seeing him again raised within her.

In fact it was well after lunch before Justin caught up with them, by which time they were in the operating-theatre, taking advantage of a lull before the afternoon list to do a reconnoitre. Penny, however, was becoming increasingly frustrated as she was asked all sorts of questions about the best place to site the cameras, about which side of the operating-table Justin would be standing, how long would the various stages of the operation take and so forth—none of which she could answer with any degree of certainty.

'Honestly!' she said finally, reaching a peak of exasperation again. 'The one person who really should be here apparently cannot spare us any of his precious time.' Hardly had the words died in her throat than the electrically operated doors of the modern theatre slid apart and his tall figure, clad in a white coat, appeared—apologising profusely for inconveniencing everybody. Indeed, so genuine was his concern that her outburst immediately seemed very out of place. She felt a sense of relief that he had not actually witnessed it.

'Never mind, I've no doubt Sister Shepherd has been filling in the details more than adequately,' he went on. Her mollification was complete at this and she started to protest, but he had embarked on a swift, bilingual description of the operation he would be performing.

'There are four stages, really,' he explained. 'As you know, the patient has suffered severe burns to the side of her face and her right hand; the one causing disfigurement and impairment of her facial muscles; the other resulting in lack of flexibility in the skin on the back of the hand. Both of these problems would inevitably end her brilliant career. However, I do not intend to let that happen. The first job is to excise the scar tissue from each site—haemostasis is now complete of course—and then I shall superimpose fresh skin on the receptor sites, using Thiersch grafts on the face and a tubed pedicle graft for the hand.' He paused and she found herself responding to his enthusiasm. Gone was the smooth veneer of the television personality, replaced by the confident dedication of the surgeon.

'What will you be using as the donor site?' she asked. She had already had the strange impression that his explanations had been mostly directed towards herself, and now her question focused his entire attention upon her.

'The abdominal wall,' he replied. 'I made the preparatory incisions for the flap some weeks ago, so it is all ready for one end to be transferred.'

'I see,' mused Penny. 'I think Angus was under the impression that everything was going to be completed tomorrow.' She turned to her colleagues to find that her surmise had been correct. Angus was practically hopping about with consternation.

'What do you mean?' he cried. 'Of course it must all be completed tomorrow! We can't possibly go over budget.'

Penny hurriedly continued. 'I don't think it's a problem, Angus. Tomorrow is the really vital part and all that will happen in a couple of weeks' time is the final transfer of the flap, once vascularisation has been adequately achieved.'

Angus looked even more mystified. 'I haven't understood a single word of all this, Penny,' he said helplessly. 'And I'm quite sure our French friends haven't either.'

'Well it's very simple really—' She stopped, realising that both she and Justin had started on an explanation at the same time. He turned to her with a warm smile and gestured for her to continue.

Encouraged, she sought in her mind for the most straightforward means to explain things. 'What Justin will have done two or three weeks ago is make a flap of skin on the patient's tummy. He's left each end of the flap attached and has sutured the cut surfaces. Just imagine a tube of skin lying there waiting, but still attached at each end. Tomorrow, he will detach one of the ends and join it to the damaged area of the hand. The hand itself will be strapped in place across the abdomen for a week or two until the replacement skin has taken root as it were—and then the other end is separated and the whole flap moulded to the size and shape required to cover the new place where it will go.'

'I see,' said Angus, still looking a little puzzled. 'But isn't that terribly uncomfortable for the patient, being strapped up like that?'

'Yes, it is,' interjected Justin, 'but she has been prepared psychologically and it is a small price to pay for having the full use of her hand back again. It's necessary to take this type of full thickness graft because it's the only sort that can cover the tendons and cortical bone which the burns exposed.'

'I see.' Angus turned and translated the general gist of this, slightly hesitantly this time and accompanied by much gesture and demonstration with his hands. His translation resulted in further questions from the French team and he turned to Penny again. 'Yes, I think we've got all that, Penny, but won't it just mean making a new scar on her stomach—and is the disfigurement on her face going to be treated in the same way?'

'Well, I think Justin will probably be taking a series of thinner patches of skin to replace the lost facial tissue and he'll also use some of those to cover the area he took the pedicled graft from. It's possible to take sheets of skin so thin as to leave the layer which can grow new skin still intact—the, er, Mal, er, Mal . . .'

'Malphygian layer,' prompted Justin. For a second she thought he was patronising her again but her side-long glance saw nothing but helpfulness in his eyes. It was rather disconcerting.

'Yes, the malphygian layer,' she repeated with a grateful smile. Angus was still looking puzzled though and she frowned, trying to find a way of making things absolutely clear. She had a sudden flash of inspiration. 'It's like having a lawn. You can cut it normally, leaving the roots intact to provide new growth, but it's as if the *cuttings* have the miraculous ability to be transplanted to repair damaged or bare patches,' she said triumphantly.

The puzzled expression on Angus's face finally cleared and he turned to the TVNF people again. A certain amount of amusement resulted from his inability to remember the French for lawn-mowing and he resorted to an exaggerated, but successful, mime.

Penny and Justin exchanged looks of relief that they had at last got through to everybody. She felt a thrill of shared achievement completely out of proportion to the circumstances. Justin was standing closely at her side and their mutual professional knowledge seemed to set them apart from the others even more. He cleared his throat abruptly and turned to her.

'I was wondering if you would care to—' he began but Angus was asking if they could just clear up a couple of final production points and his attention was diverted again. She withdrew into the background and let the discussion proceed, intensely eager to know what he had been about to ask her. It seemed a long time before he could return his attention to her, not until the party was leaving the operating-theatre, in fact. She regarded him expectantly.

'I thought you might be interested in having a look round the Marie Frambére,' he said. 'It is a very up to date clinic and their severe burns unit is using some dramatic new methods pioneered jointly with the Sharman Oaks Hospital in San Francisco. You're unlikely to see anything like it in England for some time yet.'

For one absurd moment she felt a disappointment that his invitation was only a professional one. She had thought he was about to ask her out to dinner but thrust this notion away and replied that she would be very interested indeed.

'I thought we might look in our patient as well. She's a perfectly charming person and would welcome a visit from another English girl, I know. But I'll show you the intensive care unit first.'

They made their way along the bright modern corridor. Justin was obviously a familiar figure, receiving frequent greetings as they passed members of the clinic's staff. He led her along to a viewing window. 'This is where our patient was first brought after the accident. She's moved on to a private room now. As you can see, we have another very bad case here that's just been admitted. It's a child—badly burned in a kitchen accident. Usual story, this time it was a pan of hot fat. The mother acted quickly with cold water, thank God, but it's quite severe on the trunk and arms. She was only wearing a night-gown.'

They were looking into a room with a very unusual arrangement. The patient, obviously sedated, was lying on a mattress moulded into dozens of small cones—it looked rather like an egg carton.

'That's an excellent idea,' murmured Penny. 'Presumably, the body is held off the sheets but the cones and hollows allow air to circulate around the wounds?'

'Exactly right,' he replied.

'But what's that arrangement? It looks like something out of a spacecraft!' She pointed to a large, curved shield in some clear material or other which hung over the bed. It appeared to be connected to a power supply.

'It's a plexiglass and copper heating device. It allows the patient to lie there in a controlled temperature environment without the discomfort of blankets. And you're right, it *is* a by-product of space technology. Of course, the ideal method of treating burns would be to put the patient actually in a space craft. The absence of gravity would allow him to hang in mid air not touching anything,' he smiled.

'But this technique is a fantastic advance!' she exclaimed. 'Presumably it's just as effective with exposure treatment as with pressure-dressing?'

'Indeed it is. We're using pressure-dressing here because the burns are mostly on the trunk. However,' he continued, 'we have also developed a method of pressure-dressing facial wounds—'

'But they're practically impossible to bandage!' she cried.

'Exactly, so we've developed something else,' he replied with an arch smile. 'I think it's time you met tomorrow's patient.' He strode off down the corridor again, leaving her no choice but to follow. She did so gladly, for his enthusiasm was infectious and she had become caught up in it.

Her professional training enabled her to hide any distress at seeing what terrible things the accident had done to the beautiful young girl's face. She was not, however, prepared for the odd sight which confronted her. The patient was wearing a close-fitting plastic mask. It looks like a large bubble and the strange thing was how closely it appeared to fit the contours of her face.

'It's made of lucite,' Justin explained after he had made the introductions. 'It's a new material that we can actually mould to the individual's features, leaving the nose, mouth and eyes free. The advantages are that the skin heals more quickly if it is compressed, with less scarring and a smoother texture. The transparent mask provides the pressure, but the patient can lead a fairly normal life and we can actually follow the progress visually as the skin heals. As you can see, her face is pretty well healed, apart from the scarring on the masseter muscle tissue and down across the jaw-bone and neck. Without the mask, things would have been much worse.'

They stayed chatting for a while and Justin showed her the tubed pedicle flap on the abdominal wall awaiting its transfer to the patient's hand. Penny was able to add to his reassurance of the patient about a successful out-come tomorrow. When they finally returned to the clinic's reception area, they found that Angus had left a message to say that the rest of the party had gone on to their hotel.

'I'm sorry, Penny,' Justin apologised looking at his wrist-watch. 'I didn't realise we had been so long.'

'Oh no,' she protested. 'Really, it's been very interest-ing. I wouldn't have missed it for anything. In any case, it will help me tomorrow.' He looked puzzled and she quickly explained how Angus had asked for her to be present in the control room to explain the sequence of events as the operation proceeded.

'I shall have to be at my best, then,' he exclaimed, 'with such a critical audience.' She was about to take issue with this but realised he was gently making fun of her.

'Come on,' he said. 'Let's share a taxi.'

Their hotel was situated further into the city and Penny tried to focus her attention on the passing street scene. She was very aware of his presence next to her and the bulk of his shoulder lightly touching hers. For the first time she felt relaxed in his company. It was because they had been discussing professional matters, she told herself.

They came across Tim in the hotel reception. 'I've just been for a sight-seeing walk,' he announced. 'Working up an appetite for dinner.' He paused. 'Oh, of course,

I don't expect you've heard. Our French opposite numbers have asked us out. I take it you can both come?'

'Oh, how lovely,' exclaimed Penny and turned to see Justin's reaction. He was filling in a hotel registration form with his silver pen.

'Thank you, but I shall have to decline,' he replied a little stiffly. 'I am planning to take an early night in readiness for tomorrow. I shall dine in the hotel, I think.' He looked up and stared at her. At first she thought he was being critical of the relaxed approach to things amongst the television profession. Then she had the strongest conviction that he was on the point of asking her if she would like to join him rather than go out with the others. She was confused, not knowing what to say, but soon the moment was past and the French hotel receptionist was asking her to register as well. She was given a peculiar strip of plastic which she looked at uncertainly.

'*C'est votre clef, mademoiselle*—your key,' the receptionist had explained. She nodded, not really understanding.

Tim had disappeared and she and Justin went across to the lift. Their baggage had already arrived and been taken up to their rooms.

'Which floor?' he asked, a finger poised over the lift buttons.

'It's Room 701,' she read the number on her strip of plastic. 'Must be on the seventh floor, I suppose.'

'That's both of us, then,' he observed. 'I'm Room 721.' The lift began to ascend with a soft whine. She could feel his eyes upon her and she twiddled with a button on her jacket of the linen suit, staring fixedly at the floor indicator panel. The doors slid open and they followed a room number sign. Both their rooms lay in the same direction. She stopped in front of Room 701 and realised that he had also halted. Their rooms were exactly opposite one another.

She looked at the door blankly. Not only had she been given a key which bore no resemblance to any she had ever seen before, but she could not make out anything on the door which looked like a lock.

'Here.' He had seen her confusion and gently took the plastic strip from her and slid it into a slot by the door handle. There was a buzz and a click and the door swung open.

'It's electronic,' he explained. 'Better security.' She smiled her thanks, still feeling a little foolish and peered into her room.

'Oh look,' she cried, 'there's a view.' She darted in and across to the big picture window. 'Is that the Eiffel Tower?' she asked, pointing to the skyline. He was standing in the doorway, trying to see what had caught her attention. She indicated again, aware that by doing so she was inviting him in. He came across to join her at the window, leaving the door open.

'Yes,' he said. 'That's the Eiffel Tower all right. I rather think you've got a room on the best side of the hotel.'

'Can you recognise anything else?'

'Not really. We're still some way out from the centre. I think that's the top of Notre Dame over there, but I can't really pick out anything else.'

'Oh, I should so like to go up the Eiffel Tower,' she said, 'and see the Seine and the Latin Quarter and everything.'

'You wouldn't have preferred to do some sight-seeing this afternoon?'

'Oh good heavens, no,' she protested. 'I was fascinated with the Marie Frambére. Anyway, this isn't a holiday.'

He smiled at her. 'Well, I know—but you ought to make the most of the trip. I hadn't realised it was your first visit to Paris. Perhaps tonight will be fun. Your dinner out, I mean. You like the television people, Tim and Angus and everybody, they are good company.'

'Yes, they are,' she agreed. 'But I shall also make it an early night. Like you, I want to be fresh for tomorrow. It's a shame you couldn't come, though.'

'Yes, it is. But I think it's best not to.'

'Yes. I expect you are right.'

They were facing each other now, still standing by the window. Everything suddenly seemed very intimate.

'Well,' he broke the spell, as if with some effort, and turned to make his way back across the room, 'I hope you have a good time.'

She followed him and stood with one hand on the door's edge. He turned to her again in the doorway.

'Thank you,' she replied.

'Until the morning, then.'

He regarded her intently and then, with exquisite gentleness, reached a hand to her face and cupped her chin. His gesture was hardly necessary, for she was already raising her face to his kiss. They remained apart, with just their lips touching and his hand still gently cradling her face. She closed her eyes and her senses swam. She knew nothing but the cool softness of his mouth on hers. Her lips parted and she surrendered to the languor which began to pervade her body.

And then it was over. She opened her eyes to see such tenderness in his that her emotions reeled. He walked slowly across to his room and without a backward glance, opened the door, went in and closed it behind him with a soft click. She stood there trembling and holding on to the door for what seemed an age, but could only have been seconds, her senses spinning and her legs weak.

CHAPTER TEN

THE EVENING out with TVNF had been imbued with a strange aura. She knew that it was she, Penny, who was sitting in the friendly French restaurant a few streets from the hotel, but it felt like someone else. She had the oddest feeling that she was looking down upon herself as if watching another person trying to engage in light conversation with her hosts. They had even invited along a PA from the studio to provide a female opposite number for her. Despite the girl's excellent English, Penny could only find the barest of platitudes to exchange with her. Nor could she do justice to the superb French cooking.

On the gentle stroll through the warm summer evening back to the hotel, Tim had fallen in step with her and even asked if she was feeling all right.

'You seem a little subdued,' he had said concernedly. She replied that it must be the thought of tomorrow and wanting to be sure of giving Angus all her support to make sure the best shots were taken.

Back at the reception desk she had decided to order a simple breakfast to be served in her room the next morning, saying that she was the lightest of eaters first thing. The truth, she knew, was that she could not be sure of her reaction when next she saw Justin. Somehow it would be worse being with him in the company of other people.

She had slipped into her room, casting a glance at his

door opposite. It stared back at her in the deserted hotel corridor, an impersonal barrier which seemed to be mocking her. The click of her door as she shut it was very loud in the silence.

She undressed slowly and slid down between the sheets, the cotton cool on her bare legs. It was a double bed and felt big and empty. She lay there in the dark, pictures forming in her mind of him lying asleep in the room across the corridor. Like most modern hotels, all the furnishings were alike and knowing that his room was probably a replica of hers added an extra dimension of reality to her thoughts. Perhaps he, too, was lying awake, staring at the ceiling in the warm darkness. She could imagine his dark-haired head on the white pillow, could still feel the exquisite gentleness of his lips on hers. She had stayed awake for a long time.

The morning came and pushed in on her thoughts, eclipsing the half-remembered dreams and images which had coloured her sleep. The French room-service maid knocked and entered and firmly drew the curtains to let the morning light flood in. With it came the knowledge that there were duties to be performed to-day, responsibilities to be met. Penny pulled back the bedclothes, slipped off her nightie and went into the bathroom to shower. She turned the jets full on, keeping the water lukewarm to refresh herself and letting the invigorating needles beat against her body, gasping at the sensation. She towelled herself briskly and went to pour a cup of the strong French coffee. She sipped it and stared into the distance through the big window.

She now knew with a deep, abiding certainty that she had fallen in love with him. She had never felt like this before with anyone. The last few weeks—and especially working with him—had somehow brought all the sides of his personality together into a whole which she felt she now understood very well. And it was a personality she knew was utterly irresistible. She also knew sadly that she could never compete with the sort of women that he found attractive—Helen Lampard, for example, with her sparkling conversation and mature sophistication. The memory of the day on the river returned and her eyes misted as she realised that for him it would have been just a diverting day out.

She pulled a tissue from her box and blew her nose angrily. She resolved to throw herself into today's activities and then firmly withdraw from all contact with him. Perhaps she should have taken Karen's advice and simply returned to a post at St Vincent's. A bittersweet certainty lingered, however, that she was glad she had not—no matter what the consequences had been.

Meeting everybody in reception later, she experienced the familiar mixture of disappointment and relief that Justin was not present. He had apparently breakfasted early and already gone across to the Marie Frambére.

When they arrived in the mobile control room, Angus began flapping as usual. Once more she went through the sequence of the operation with him, only partially managing to calm him down. It was understandable she told herself, for the atmosphere in the control room was laced with suspense. There were several people present and she was warmly greeted by the French director and his PA. Angus was to sit at his side and she next to Angus.

They were in contact with the operating-theatre not only through two cameramen, but also through a floor manager with a radio microphone. Penny stared across the banks of controls and switches at the flickering screens as a voice crackled over the loudspeakers in French. Angus leaned across to her.

'Apparently Justin is scrubbed now and we're practically ready to go,' he said. She looked back at the screens and watched the doors of the theatre slide back to allow someone to enter. A picture switched into extreme close-up, jumped, then steadied and pulled back. She felt her heart lurch—for a second she had been looking into Justin's eyes from the same distance as her last encounter with him in the doorway to her room. This time though, they were separated by a barrier of television technology. She dragged her attention back to Angus as the operation got under way.

She watched, fascinated, as his skilful fingers performed the excisional surgery to remove the scar tissue from face and neck. He had decided on a general anaesthetic, largely because of the length of time that would be involved and the risk of patient fatigue.

The minutes ticked by, gradually becoming hours. The atmosphere in the control room had become calm, reflecting that of the operating theatre, where Justin's quiet confidence seemed to permeate everything. The French director was interspersing shots of Justin's hands with close-ups of his face. The steel-blue eyes hardly blinked, his concentration absolute as he began the delicate process of taking the Thiersch graft from the skin surface of the stomach.

'He'll probably start with a fairly large graft to cover the cheek damage and then work down across the jaw-line, using the postage stamp method,' she murmured to Angus.

'Sorry?' he asked.

'He'll probably take smaller and smaller grafts—possibly down to only two centimetres square,' she explained. 'And on the neck, he'll replace tissue up to the Langer's lines. They're the natural creases in the skin,' she added. 'If he can close the wound along those lines, the scarring is reduced.'

They watched in silence, broken only by the director's instructions to the cameramen as Justin began the task of restoring the patient's face. He worked painstakingly, with meticulous care, transferring the patches of precious tissue with infinite gentleness, all the time issuing quiet instructions to the theatre staff.

Soon the process of grafting was complete and he replaced the lucite mask which Penny had seen the patient wearing. She suggested Angus filmed this from a number of angles, explaining that it represented a breakthrough in the pressure-dressing of facial areas. She heard Justin calling for a report from the anaesthetist and saw him glance at the operating-theatre clock.

'He is going to complete the graft on the hand, isn't he?' Angus was becoming agitated again. 'The tubed—what did he call it?'

'Tubed pedicle,' replied Penny. 'And don't worry, I'm sure he is. In fact, although it seems more complicated, it is actually simpler. Look, they're positioning the patient's arm now so that he can transfer one end of the graft.'

Angus subsided into a tense silence and they watched as the long and difficult operation was brilliantly brought to its conclusion. She felt like applauding as the patient was wheeled out and she heard instructions being issued to lock off the cameras and cut the video recording.

Justin looked directly at a camera and she saw his eyes smile above the mask and a hand raised in the thumbs-up sign. He disappeared through the theatre doors towards the surgeon's dressing area.

'I'm going to go and congratulate him,' declared Angus, jumping to his feet. 'Come on, Penny.'

They found him in one of the theatre ante-rooms, sitting back in a chair, his long legs raised to prop his feet up on a cabinet. He was still wearing his gown but had pulled his cap from his head and tugged the mask down beneath his chin. Despite the length and intensity of what he had just done, there was little sign of strain on the lean face. A nurse was giving him a cup of coffee. He gave Angus and Penny a lazy smile, his eyes holding hers for far longer than was necessary. She felt her heart turn over.

'How did it look?' he asked and they answered in delighted unison that everything had been perfect.

'Excellent,' he said and his eyes returned to Penny. For a second, she was positive that he was wishing Angus was not with them. She searched for a fresh subject of conversation.

'What's the next stage?' she enquired of both of them.

'Well, I'm hoping to do a very rough first edit this afternoon over at TVNF,' replied Angus. 'As a matter of fact, Penny, I was hoping you could come and see the rushes as well.'

'Yes, of course,' she said, although she felt a pang of disappointment. She had hoped that this afternoon would be free to do a little shopping, perhaps some sight-seeing too.

'I can't, I'm afraid,' Justin was saying. 'There are a few odds and ends to take care of here at the clinic and I have some correspondence to do. I'm sure Penny can give you all the help you need. I imagine I'll see you at the airport check-in. What time's our flight again?'

'Seven-thirty. We need to leave the hotel with our baggage by six, I believe.' Angus was agitatedly turning to leave and she followed, feeling unaccountably dismal.

By the end of the afternoon she was in almost as bad a state as Angus. To her, the recorded pictures looked absolutely perfect, but he kept asking for re-runs and was finding it very difficult to decide which takes to use. His nervousness was very wearing and by the time they were due to go back to the hotel to pack, she was exhausted. She had completely forgotten his phobia about flying as well, until he reminded her of it with several apprehensive comments in the taxi. She decided to find Justin and ask if he had any mild tranquillisers for Angus, but when she reached his door, it was open and the room had a deserted, empty air. He must have gone to the airport straight from the Marie Frambère.

At the airport check-in, she searched anxiously for him and located his tall figure at the Air France desk with a great deal of relief. She reached his side a little breathlessly. He turned and his face lit up to see her.

'Hallo, Penny. I was just asking if you'd already checked in. There's a window seat free next to me in the non-smoking section. Would you like to take it?'

She hesitated, diverted for a moment from her concern about Angus. 'Well, yes, that would be very pleasant.'

'Good.' He turned to the check-in girl again and Penny wondered if she were making too much fuss. She saw Angus making his way over to them, pushing a trolley with their baggage from the taxi. A look at his face made her gasp. It was ashen, beads of perspiration starting from his forehead along the hairline. She caught a glimpse of the expression in his eyes. It was a chilling, hunted sort of look. She tugged at Justin's arm, pulling him away from his conversation at the desk. He registered Angus's appearance in an instant.

'Angus, are you all right?' He stepped forward, but Angus had stopped stock-still and was gripping his shoulder.

'Feel dreadful,' he was muttering. 'Terrible pain in my arm.'

For a moment, the three of them stood transfixed, like a set piece in a tableau. Then Angus gave a hoarse cry and pitched forward, sending the baggage trolley spinning and the cases flying. People around them backed away as if from sudden danger. A woman screamed.

Justin leaped forward to the side of the prostrate body and turned Angus over. His fingers slid into the neck of his open shirt, feeling for the carotid pulse and his other hand lifted back the eyelids. He turned his head, seeking Penny.

'My bag,' he snapped. 'It's on the weigh-in.' He gestured with his head to the airline desk and she dashed to grab the leather flight-bag. 'There's a spare stethoscope,' he said. She was kneeling opposite him, Angus between them, and delved in the bag. It was full of toilet items, spare clothes, a camera, notebooks.

'I can't—'

'I think it's in the side pocket.'

She found the stethoscope and thrust it into his hand. He positioned it and grasped the chest-piece. Penny's fingers were already undoing Angus's shirt buttons. He listened briefly and then looked up again.

'Cardiac arrest,' he said tersely. 'Can you do the mouth-to-mouth? I'll apply pressure to the sternum.' He looked up at the circle of faces around them, all registering that sort of mesmerised mixture of shock and dull fascination with which the public invariably witness emergencies. His eyes found an airline ground-staff girl.

'We need space round here—and an ambulance,' he barked—and then in exasperation at the lack of response, '*Une ambulance! Vite!*'

The scene changed and people shot off in different directions. He and Penny set to work. She had pulled off the jacket from her blue linen suit and, folding it into a pillow, unceremoniously thrust it under Angus's neck. For what seemed an age, they strove against time, he applying double-palmed pressure on the breast-bone, while she alternated with deep exhalations of air into Angus's mouth. Periodically they paused and Justin listened intently through the stethoscope. The seconds ticked by, slowly becoming minutes. Suddenly, his eyes widened.

'A flicker,' he exclaimed. 'Keep up the mouth-to-mouth.' He applied sternum massage again. Then he listened for longer and gradually his expression, tensed with suspense, began to relax.

'Cardiac re-start,' he murmured to her. 'Let's just hope it was quick enough.' She applied another exhalation, seeing out of the corner of her eye Angus's chest rise in time to her effort. She straightened up again and they both watched. Yes, there was a definite movement now, only just discernible, but definitely Angus's own. They waited for several minutes to make sure the situation had stabilised, then turned him over into the recovery position.

'I'll go and find out what's happening to that ambulance,' he said and shouldered his way off through the crowd. Two airport security men had reached the scene by now and were making a moderate success of keeping people moving.

The events which followed had a dream-like quality. There was never any question but that they should both travel in the ambulance with Angus to the local hospital, that she should smooth over the administrative formalities of admitting him, that Justin should confer with the French A and E doctor about the case. As with many emergencies, events seemed to telescope into a very short space of time. She was amazed to see that her watch registered only eight o'clock as she sat in the hospital waiting-room. She looked up and with some relief saw Justin returning with a reassuring smile on his face. She rose to her feet.

'How is he?' she enquired urgently.

'He's going to be OK.' He had raised his arms and rested both his hands on her shoulders.

'Thank God,' she breathed. He gently turned her and they both sat down, both sharing the feeling of intense relief. One of his arms continued to rest along her shoulder and it was very easy to lean her head to one side and rest it inside the crook of his elbow. They sat together in an atmosphere of friendly intimacy for several minutes.

'Poor Angus,' she said. 'I just knew he was leading up to a coronary. He never relaxes.'

'No. A classic personality type,' he agreed. 'Still, he'll be all right, but he'll have to change his way of life. There's no brain damage and with care he should be able to go on for years.'

'Not in television, he won't.'

'No,' he agreed. 'Not in television.' He fell silent and seemed to be brooding over something. 'But,' he said eventually, 'the problem is, what are *we* going to do?'

'I'm sorry, I don't understand.'

'Well, I mean about tonight.'

'Tonight?'

'Yes. That was the last flight to London, you know. The one we were booked on, I mean.'

'Oh, I see.' Her mind tried to take in the implications. 'You mean we're . . .'

'Stranded together in Paris? Yes I'm rather afraid we are.' He sounded very despondent.

'Oh dear. I am sorry,' she said, making an attempt to break free from his encircling arm, but he restrained her.

'*I'm* not sorry at all,' he said. 'In fact, I can't think of a nicer thing to have happened.' He paused. 'All that we need is to discover that miraculously our baggage has been returned to our hotel, that they have let us keep our rooms for an extra night, and that a table is booked for us at my favourite restaurant in Montmartre.'

This time she really did manage to break free, but could see only a sort of agonised suspense in his eyes.

'Well?' he said. 'Would all that appeal to you?'

'Oh yes, Justin, very much indeed, but—'

'Good,' he said, the blue eyes twinkling, 'because I have just made three telephone calls to arrange exactly that!'

The restaurant he had brought her to was tucked into a little cobbled courtyard. He had asked the taxi to drop them some way away and they had picked their route up the narrow, sloping streets. The air had been warm and gentle and all around them was the awakening Parisian night-life.

She had dressed with care, deciding in the end on her simple black dress with its neat silver belt which echoed the fine silver chain at her throat. Her new, classic black court shoes looked well with everything and she had brought a jacket in case it turned cool. They were sitting at a secluded corner table. It was all very French. The table-cloth was in a bright red and white check cotton and the centre-piece included a candle floating in a bowl of water which contained the blooms of summer flowers.

He helped her with the menu without making her feel in any way awkward over her rusty French. The candle-light reflected in his eyes as he looked at her and she hoped she looked as attractive as he did. It was a fish restaurant and he tried to coax her to join him in having oysters as an hors-d'oeuvre, but she settled for a delicious pâté, followed by *sole bonne femme*. He ordered a delightfully chilled white burgundy to accompany the delicious food.

As they lingered through the courses, he told her about how he planned to bring the facilities at Orford up to the standards of the Marie Frambére and how he intended to specialise more and more in the treatment of burns. She realised he had no intention of going much further with his television career. It was simply a rather entertaining diversion.

As he talked, she knew she had never been so happy in another person's company in all her life. The familiar voice of caution which still echoed inside was now very faint indeed as it warned her against giving in to the insane images which were chasing through her mind, images of them both together and alone, of him taking her in his arms, taking possession of her—and her desire being nothing but sweet surrender. She did not care any more about being sensible, about the love affairs he must have had, about the other women very different to herself that he knew. She did not even care that this night with him in Paris, so unexpected yet somehow so predestined, was all she would ever have. It did not matter at all, for at this moment it was enough.

So engrossed were they with each other that they did not realise that they were the last people left in the restaurant until they became aware of the waiter hovering by their table.

'I rather think we must go,' he smiled and signalled for the bill. With a sad sense of finality she watched him pay and thank the waiter.

Outside it was cooler and she draped her jacket around her shoulders.

'The night is still very young,' he murmured. 'Would you care to walk a little? There is something I would like to show you.' She nodded smilingly and they began to stroll. After a while, he slipped his arm round her waist and she did the same to him, feeling the hardness of his body next to her as they walked.

They passed other restaurants, some still busy—and the occasional night-club, with different strains of music drifting out across the cobbled streets. People who lived in the area were to be seen on their balconies, often with friends, seated around tables sharing a bottle of wine. From one open window the strains of ballet music floated down from a record player or radio. It was Tchaikovsky's *Sleeping Beauty*.

'You enjoy the ballet, don't you?' she asked suddenly, wanting yet not wanting to hear his reply.

'Yes,' he said, stopping for an instant and looking down at her. 'How did you know?'

She resumed walking, looking down at her feet. 'Oh, I saw you at Covent Garden once, you didn't see me. It was a performance of *Cinderella*.

'Covent Garden? But that was only last month. Why didn't you say hello?' He sounded puzzled.

'You were with someone. Helen, is it?'

'Oh yes, that's right.' He chuckled. 'Dear old Helen.'

They walked on for a while. 'I expect she's a very special friend?' she ventured.

'Oh yes, rather. Known her for years, her husband was my best friend. He died suddenly a few years ago. Knocked poor Helen sideways. I've been trying to put her back together. She wouldn't go out at all until I managed to persuade her to come on the river. She's much better now and has given me all sorts of advice. In fact it was she who first got me interested in *Life Lines* in the first place. She knows Jeremy Wheeler very well. So you could say she brought you and me together, in a funny sort of way.'

Penny's heart was pounding, the images in her mind now completely out of control. They had emerged from the side streets of Montmartre and she saw a beautiful old building rising up before them. It was softly lit, the ancient stones blending together in tones of light and shade.

'It's the church of Sacré Coeur,' he breathed in her ear. 'It's one of my favourite buildings in Paris.' He turned. 'But this is what I wanted to show you.' He led her down some steps and over to a stone wall. She looked out and saw that their climb had brought them up to a vantage point high above the city. She could see the

Eiffel Tower in its floodlights quite clearly and many more lighted landmarks against the velvety summer darkness, although her thoughts would not stand still enough for her to attempt to name them.

He had turned to her and, placing his hands on her waist, gently drew her to him. Her arms lifted to slip up behind his neck, the jacket falling unheeded to the ground. Their lips met and she melted against him. After a long time, they broke apart and she turned her head into his shoulder, looking out again at the lights of the city spread before them.

'I am so glad you approve of the view,' he whispered. She laughed and felt his arms tighten round her again.

'From where I am standing I would say that it is a remarkably nice view,' she replied softly. There was a long silence.

'Tell me, Penny, is it a view you might consider having on a permanent basis? I would like to know now please, for I have fallen very much in love with you.'

She closed her eyes and stayed very quietly with her head still resting against his shoulder.

'Oh yes, Justin,' she replied seriously. 'I should like that a great deal. In fact, I don't think there has ever really been any doubt about it.'

Doctor Nurse Romances

Amongst the intense emotional pressures of modern medical life, doctors and nurses often find romance. Read about their lives and loves in the other three Doctor Nurse titles· available this month.

PRODIGAL DOCTOR
by Lynne Collins

*All starch and no heart…*That's Dr Eliot Hailey's verdict on his wife, Sister Claudia Hailey, when they're thrown together after a four-year separation. Having given up hopes of a home and husband, Claudia has dedicated herself to nursing — but will Eliot's sudden reappearance change her mind?

THE HEALING PROCESS
by Grace Read

'I'm quite capable of running my own life without advice from *you*,' Staff Nurse Nicky Pascall tells Dr Alex Baron. But if she is to recover from her broken heart, perhaps his tender loving care is the best way to start the healing process.

DREAMS ARE FOR TOMORROW
by Frances Crowne

In the depths of despair with her love-life and her work, Nurse Fleur Hamilton finds herself pouring out her troubles on the sympathetic shoulders of Dr Antoine Devos. Next morning, filled with embarrassment, her only comfort is that at least she'll never have to see him again…will she?

Mills & Boon
the rose of romance

4 Doctor Nurse Romances
FREE

Coping with the daily tragedies and ordeals of a busy hospital, and sharing the satisfaction of a difficult job well done, people find themselves unexpectedly drawn together. Mills & Boon Doctor Nurse Romances capture perfectly the excitement, the intrigue and the emotions of modern medicine, that so often lead to overwhelming and blissful love. By becoming a regular reader of Mills & Boon Doctor Nurse Romances you can enjoy EIGHT superb new titles every two months plus a whole range of special benefits: your very own personal membership card, a free newsletter packed with recipes, competitions, bargain book offers, plus big cash savings.

AND an Introductory FREE GIFT for YOU.
Turn over the page for details.

**Fill in and send this coupon back today
and we'll send you
4 Introductory
Doctor Nurse Romances yours to keep**

FREE

At the same time we will reserve a
subscription to Mills & Boon
Doctor Nurse Romances for you. Every
two months you will receive the latest
8 new titles, delivered direct to your door.
You don't pay extra for delivery. Postage and
packing is always completely Free.
There is no obligation or commitment –
you receive books only for
as long as you want to.

It's easy! Fill in the coupon below and return it to
**MILLS & BOON READER SERVICE, FREEPOST, P.O. BOX 236,
CROYDON, SURREY CR9 9EL.**

Please note: READERS IN SOUTH AFRICA write to
**Mills & Boon Ltd., Postbag X3010,
Randburg 2125, S. Africa.**

FREE BOOKS CERTIFICATE

**To: Mills & Boon Reader Service, FREEPOST, P.O. Box 236,
Croydon, Surrey CR9 9EL.**

Please send me, free and without obligation, four Dr. Nurse Romances, and reserve a
Reader Service Subscription for me. If I decide to subscribe I shall receive, following my free
parcel of books, eight new Dr. Nurse Romances every two months for £8.00, post and
packing free. If I decide not to subscribe, I shall write to you within 10 days. The free books
are mine to keep in any case. I understand that I may cancel my subscription at any time
simply by writing to you. I am over 18 years of age.
Please write in BLOCK CAPITALS.

Name _____

Address _____

_____

_____ Postcode _____

SEND NO MONEY — TAKE NO RISKS

EP11